The Swine's Wedding

Daniel Evan Weiss

HIGH RISK BOOKS

NEW YORK / LONDON

Library of Congress Catalog Card Number: 96–68815

First published in 1996 by
Serpent's Tail, 180 Varick Street, 10th floor, New York, NY 10014,
and in 1997 by Serpent's Tail, 4 Blackstock Mews, London N4 2BT

Cover design by Rex Ray
Phototypeset in Janson, Helvetica and Courier by Intype London Ltd
Printed in Finland by Werner Söderström Oy

For Katy

AUTHOR'S NOTE

In the interest of saving readers time, I have compressed some minor details of the Spanish and Portuguese Inquisitions and their consequences. However, the essential facts are all too true; I have been careful to neither magnify nor minify the astonishing temper of that time.

FIRE AND INCIDENT REPORT

Bureau of Fire Investigation Job Number 62—4013
Incident location: 348 Broadwell Ave.
Incident date: June 14
Incident time: 12:10 PM
Day of week: Saturday
Weather: Clear, 72 degrees
Structural information: Residential, one
family, two storey, wood frame
Owner of structure: Mrs. Miriam Beneviste
Fire marshal assigned: M. J. Hazel
Origin and extension: Examination showed that fire
originated in the basement of the subject
premise. Fire extended up multiple channels.
First floor was quickly consumed, and fire
continued up to second floor. Roof caught fire and
collapsed, as did east, south, and west walls.
The fire was thereto extinguished.
Remarks: Initial efforts to extinguish blaze were
delayed by woman dressed in wedding gown who was
standing beside residence. Paramedics had to
remove her from scene.

INTERVIEW SHEET

Complaint—Follow up Information
Preliminary Investigation and Interviews of BFI
Job Number 62—4013

1. Dispatcher #16 reported a 10—45—2 at 12.15 hours. Second fire company responded.
2. Company reported heavy black smoke issuing from house. Heavy volume of fire, colored yellow-white, seen through basement windows, indicating unusual heat from such a structure. Heavy volume of fire colored yellow-orange seen through windows of first floor. Smell of hydrocarbon accelerant, probably gasoline, reported.
3. Lieutenant stated that when he approached house the front porch and doorway were fully involved in fire. He found back door and porch fully involved. Fire was coming from all first storey windows, and from all second storey windows except on the north wall. Dense smoke from attic soffit vents indicated fire in attic.
4. Resident's car was parked in front of house. Lights inside house were on when company arrived, and went out soon after. Lieutenant and his forcible entry man broke through front door but house was heavily charged with smoke and he could not see anything. Extreme heat forced them to retreat from structure.
5. Roof and three walls collapsed. Fire was

extinguished at 15.35 hours. Personnel then
entered. Three bodies, badly burned, were found
in the middle of the basement. They were removed.
Lieutenant transmitted a 10—45—1, DOA.

INTERVIEW SHEET

Complaint—Follow up Information
Preliminary Investigation and Interviews of BFI
Job Number 62—4013

1. Paramedic team #6 arrived at scene of fire four minutes after fire company. Fire personnel put in their charge a woman found at scene.
2. Paramedics stated that woman was Caucasian, 25—30 years old, approximately 5 ft. 7 inches in height and 125 pounds. She was not carrying identification.
3. The woman was standing on the front lawn very close to the fire. She resisted attempts to move her to safety. She was moved by personnel and secured in ambulance.
4. Woman was dressed in white bridal gown. Her veil was singed and browned from fire, and rolled back over her head. There was soot on her face.
5. Woman did not speak. Possible smoke inhalation.
6. Woman was taken to Mt. Sinai Hospital.
7. Woman was carrying a journal. Investigator on scene stated that journal belonged to Miriam Beneviste, resident of burned house. Journal could place this woman inside house at time of fire.

SEARCH WARRANT

1. County Court
Honorable LaVie MacDonald, Judge
2. To any police officer of the #3 department.
3. You are hereby authorized and directed to
search for and to seize the following property:
Any material relevant to the investigation of the
fatal fire at 348 Broadwell Avenue on June 14,
including but not limited to letters, diaries,
journals, or other documents.
4. You are authorized and directed to search the   5
following premises: Domicile of Allison
Pennybaker: 374 Sherwood Rd., Apt. 3.

EEEEE! SOLLY proposed! I keep pinching myself to be sure this is real. The blood I drew with my fingernails is real. And look in that mirror. I know that overbite anywhere. I must be Mrs. Solomon Beneviste. Or just about.

I can't believe it! I mean, we've been talking about it. Actually, I've been talking about it, but I had no idea he was listening. So here it is 3:30 in the morning, too late to call anyone! Of all the rotten luck!

I'm writing this down, in case Solly forgets while he's sleeping, or wakes up and thinks it was all a dream.

This is the record of the evening: Solomon Beneviste, earth's most wonderful man, walked in after work smelling of some kind of drink. It was mild by Pennybaker standards, but still, he doesn't drink. That was my cue. I missed it.

He started talking about work, something about mergers and acquisitions. I didn't even realize he was talking to me, and not just talking to wind down. Should I have seen this, Solly and me as a merger or an acquisition? Solly doesn't talk like that. He talks wine and roses. (Or maybe just roses.) He must have been nervous.

He came to bed about two hours after me, and he woke me up, and that never happens. What actually woke me was the heat from his chest. He was burning. I could feel it even though he wasn't touching me. When I opened my eyes he was over me, just staring at me. His arms started shaking.

He kissed me. Little tender kisses, like he was taking my lips prisoner with his, one at a time. Delicious! He covered me with kisses, over my belly, and, well, I thought he was going to kill me, he was teasing me for so long. (Mother, close this diary at once!) Then he stopped, about thirty seconds too soon. Torture! I was about to protest, but he took this weird breath. Finally I realized something was up.

He said, "I love you absolutely, cosmically, cataclysmically. Be mine."

This was the moment I've been waiting for all my life. And what did I say? "What exactly are we talking about here?" I think I knew what was happening, but I wasn't absolutely sure, and can you imagine the humiliation if I accepted and he wasn't asking?

"Marry me. Please."

Warm drops were landing on me. I thought it was sweat, since he was up there for a long time. But then I realized it was tears. He is the most amazing man.

I said yes, but I said it so hard that it came out Yehng! Like when deaf people speak.

He fell onto me, and it was just like they say in books. The earth moved! While I was lying there afterwards he reached over and then I felt cold metal on my finger. I waited until he fell asleep to come out here and look. A matter of three years of so. It's drop-dead! I mean gorgeous! The light flaming out of the rock makes you avert your eyes.

So here I am, at 3:30 in the morning, poking my diamond into my arm, trying to be sure both of us are real. Ouch! Maybe so.

INTERVIEW SHEET

Complaint—Follow up Information
Interviews of BFI Job Number 62—4013
Investigator: C. Hirschon

1. Emergency room nurse at Mt.. Sinai hospital
stated that Mrs. Louise Pennybaker entered at
18.20 looking for her daughter. She identified
woman in bridal dress brought in from fire by
paramedics as her daughter, Allison Pennybaker.
2. Nurse stated that Allison Pennybaker did not
speak to her mother or anyone else.
3. Louise Pennybaker said that Allison was
supposed to have been married this afternoon to
Solomon Beneviste at the Church of the Ascension.

LET ME TRY THIS again, in the hard light of day. Solomon charged through the door, as if he had summoned his resolve just outside and had to deliver his piece before his nerve betrayed him. He said he had done it, and I asked what.

—You know.

—How could I possibly know.

Now he hesitated, and I had to push him to continue. He started doing a strange little waltz around the room. He said— This is hard for me.

—Since when is it hard to talk to your mother?

He took my hand. He said—The family name will live on after us.

—You bought me a gravestone?

—Mama! I'm getting married.

From his odd behavior I figured he was going to say something like this. But it was a surprise. I knew that he and Allison had been spending a lot of time together, but I hadn't heard even a hint about marriage. She isn't really his type, at least not the type he has always introduced me to. They were all flashy and shapely, whereas Allison has that curious Protestant epicene quality. She might have been more attractive as a boy. But never mind all that.

He said—Is that all right?

—If that were a real question, you would have asked me sooner. I imagine you want me to tell you that this is a wonderful idea.

—Exactly.

I said—Why do you want to get married?

—Why? Well, we're in love.

I had never heard him say this about any woman, except me. Good for him. I said—Is that all?

—Isn't that enough?

—Not nearly.

—We want to have a family.

—Are you quite sure? That's a lot of responsibility.

—I think so. Is anyone ever completely sure?

—Is your family imminent?

—Mama!

—I was just wondering about the suddenness of this.

—I thought you would be happy. Don't you want grand-children?

Grandchildren! I don't even like the word. And it's hard for me to imagine someone called Grandma lying with a man.

He tried to kiss me, but I pushed him away. He was smiling that full, beautiful, innocent smile that reminded me of his father. It made my heart ache. I said—All right, tell me about it.

—It wasn't a difficult decision. It's been coming for a while.

—I mean the proposal.

—Oh. It was pretty traditional.

—I hope you were on your knees. A woman is owed that respect.

—Of course I was.

—Was it a beautiful moment? You'll never do it again.

—It was the most beautiful moment of my life, Mama.

I made him leave, and the moment he cleared the threshold I started to cry.

I NEVER GOT to sleep. I'm buzzing like I drank a pot of coffee, and I haven't had a drop. A hundred times I went into the bedroom to wake up Solly. I was dying to tell SOMEONE the great news, and he was the only one available. I watched him sleep, wondering how he could at a time like this. It's a good thing he's so good to look at.

I tried out a new signature: Allison Beneviste. It looks so much better than Pennybaker. This one has class. Beneviste. And my new initials: A. B. A&P made me sound like a grocery store. AB are the first two letters. Even before BC, which was a long time ago. At about 5 a.m. that made a lot of sense.

I went out jogging at about 6. That helped me wait to until 7:30 to call Mother and Dad.

I said hello and Mother said, "What's wrong, dear?" I told her, and she shrieked so loudly I was worried she would blow out Dad's hearing aid. Of course Dad got all alarmed and Mother had to stop me to calm him down.

Mother's first question: did we set a date. Not if I love the guy. Finally she got around to asking if the proposal was romantic. I began to tell her, but I started to laugh at the details, and I had to put my hand over the phone. I said, "It was incredible."

She said, "Did I ever tell you how your father proposed to me?"

I could hear Daddy say, "Oh Christ."

"It was beautiful. It was on my parents' porch, on a June evening. He was in his seersucker suit. He brought me daisies. He took my hand . . ."

I took the phone away from my ear and let her go on. It was the only way to respect Daddy's privacy. And it was just like her to hog my big moment.

Mother said, "Well, there's so much to do. We'll have to have a dress made. My sister knows a wonderful place. And the invitations, and the church, and I'll have to tell Father Phillips. He'll be thrilled. We're going to be very busy. It's going to be fun."

I was looking at the bedroom door and thinking about getting into bed with Solly.

That would be great fun.

Finally Daddy took the phone and asked when I'm going to see Sol again. Today?

"Yes, Daddy, I'm pretty sure."

"We'd like to welcome him to the family. Why don't you arrange something."

Eventually Solly woke up and came into the kitchen. He looked a little worn. I made him his regular breakfast: black bread, cheese, and Linguica, that hot sausage. How he can eat this in the morning is one of those great cultural mysteries.

He didn't say anything while he ate, and that made me uncomfortable. I don't know where I got this, but I had this terrible fear that the sunlight was going to make the whole thing disappear, like a puddle. So I said, "I had a great time last night."

"Me, too."

"Anything in particular you want to say about it?"

He took a sip of coffee. "I wouldn't want to be indiscreet."

"Indiscreet?"

"Maybe I'm thinking of something else."

I couldn't believe this. "You don't remember anything you could talk about without being indiscreet?"

"Gentlemen don't talk about such things."

"What things? These things?" I pushed my ring in front of his eyes. Did he forget this?

"Gentlemen never discuss manicures before noon."

But then he laughed. He stood up and put his arms out and I jumped into them.

SOLOMON INVITED me to dine with him and Allison this evening. I was a few minutes late to the restaurant, and the two of them were vigilantly watching the door as I came in. Odd. I remember that the night of my engagement the earth could have moved into another orbit and I wouldn't have noticed.

Allison had tried to add a third dimension to her limp hair, but it had defeated her. Still, I appreciate that she tried to look good for me.

I congratulated her and kissed her on the cheeks three times. This was a mistake; not versed in the custom, she butted me on the forehead. She has a hard little head, this one.

How could I set her at ease? I offered her the use of my first name, but she doesn't seem comfortable with it. Should I ask her to call me Mother? I'm sure I don't look anything like her mother.

She didn't say much until I asked her about the wedding plans. Apparently she and her mother have worked out the entire affair in one day—as far as I know. The way she spoke, it was as if her family were preparing to absorb my son like a huge amoeba. She said that the ceremony would be held at the church she and her family have attended since she was a child, where she was baptised, where she sang in the choir, and where her mother is an official of some kind and still does a lot of community work. This seemed to be news to Solomon, but he had nothing to say. He looked completely ridiculous with a martini in his hand.

Then there was the matter of her dress. They know a dressmaker who makes the most beautiful creations, and she's very excited about it, but hers won't be too lavish, which wouldn't be right with so much poverty in the world. Then she told us that the reception will be in the Highland Club (her parents' haunt for thirty-five years), which is beautiful and rustic and has wonderful food (what about all the hunger in the world?), and which has the Keiffer-Corrigan Jazz Quintet (what about all the silence in the world?). They played at her brother's wedding. But she doesn't want it to be too large—

13

no more than 200 guests. The Highland Club is also exclusive. I wonder if they've thought about that.

I said—And what can I do?

—We just want the honor of your presence.

—But I want to participate. This is my only child. I'm not a great cook, I admit, but there are many things I do quite well.

—Really, Mrs. Beneviste—Miriam—I am an only daughter. My mother has been looking forward to this all my life.

Solomon nodded as if to say, Great! But I didn't feel that way at all. The event was slipping away from me on the first day.

Solomon said—I have a great idea. You used to wonder about the Beneviste family tree. Why don't you draw it now. This is the perfect time, just before the name passes on to the next generation.

It's an interesting idea. Though I don't know if it's an appropriate wedding present, since Allison didn't respond to the suggestion, and I have no reason to think that she would care one way or the other. And I really would like to do something with a more immediate practical impact on the wedding. But I didn't want to push them on this festive day.

On the way out of the restaurant Allison pulled me aside. She said—I want you to know, Mrs. Beneviste, that I know you love Solly very much, and he adores you, and I think it's wonderful. I love him with all my heart. I'm going to do everything I can to make him happy. I feel like the luckiest woman in the world.

She kissed me once, and then I got my head out of the way.

The Lord only knows how I despise the name Solly. But she left me with a good feeling. It wasn't an easy thing for her to say to me. Does she love him? Does she know what love is? Does Solomon? Perhaps some day they will know. In the meantime, I do believe that we are going to be on the same side—or at least not on opposite sides—and that is a relief.

SOLLY MADE PLANS with his mother tonight. I wanted to see her, even though she makes me nervous. All I want from her is a fair chance.

She was at least half an hour late to the restaurant. Normally I wouldn't mind. But I did my hair up for her and my curls were all falling out by the time she showed up. I looked like I was trying to insult her. Solly said, "Don't worry about it. In families all you see is bathrobes and slippers anyway."

I couldn't imagine Mrs. Beneviste in bathrobe and slippers. Either in some elegant get-up, or naked. And she would look great either way. Now I was worrying that my body isn't as good as hers, and it isn't. I'm not as pretty. I'm not womanly enough to bear a grandson because I'm too skinny. That part isn't true—I had an abortion with Billy. But I wasn't going to win her heart bringing that up at dinner. This is what I was doing to myself just waiting for her for thirty minutes.

Solly was drinking a martini. It's painful to watch. He hates the taste, so he was taking little gulps and closing his eyes. I hope he doesn't think he has to turn into a big-time drinker to get along with my family. Though I guess it wouldn't hurt.

Mrs. Beneviste finally came in. She took me by the shoulders and kissed me over and over. I tried to kiss her back, but when I did it she cracked me forehead to forehead, like a pro wrestler. I hope that's not the regular Beneviste greeting.

She looked absolutely beautiful. She was wearing a black dress that showed her off without seeming to. She almost always wears black, Solly said. She's been doing it as long as he can remember.

And now, as always, the transformation. He was in her force field. God bless the incest taboo. I can't believe I just wrote that. But really, I could not win this contest.

She welcomed me to the family and asked me to call her Miriam. Maybe Lady Miriam.

We didn't talk all that much at dinner. I'm not sure why. I told her a little about the wedding plans, but she didn't seem all that interested. Mother and I are going to take care of the whole thing. She said she wants to help, but I think she was relieved she

15

doesn't have to. I don't think she would enjoy it. She's more of an intellectual.

At the end I told her that I really love Solly. I do. I really love him. I hope she gets to like the idea.

IT DOESN'T OFFEND me that they don't want my help with the wedding arrangements. Certainly a woman like Louise Pennybaker, who has devoted her life to the practice of home economics, is more skillful than I, who have languished in my library of art, history, and classical literature. Who am I to intrude on the confection of a huge, bland cake, most of which will end up in the pocketbooks of old ladies, destined for their maids and dogs? Nor am I qualified to insist that invitations absolutely must be colored off-white shade 17, "tepid peach hangover." I could never make little crustless white bread sandwiches, or press little muck-sucking creatures from the sea bottom into pristine Protestant pastries.

All right, I admit it. I wouldn't be much help with the wedding arrangements. I just wanted them to ask me. That's not evil.

It seems so excessive. You vow your eternal loyalty and love to each other before God, and if He decides you are to be blessed, the way Aaron and I were, you find out later that night, when you're alone in bed (and not a moment earlier). If you're not, all the photographers and the bridesmaids and the hairdressers and the dressmakers and the caterers in the world don't mean a damn. A big, glossy photo album is like a totem. If there is no God in the marriage, it has no power.

17

I WENT HOME after work. Mother already has a pile of catalogs and brides' magazines, with paper clips on the chosen pages. The news is only two days old. I'm still a little afraid it's not real.

We sat in the kitchen with Dad. Mother said, "I spoke with Father Phillips yesterday. He would love you to stop in and see him."

Father Phillips takes my hand and starts talking and there's no way out. It's like a taste of eternity. Is that too strong? I like him. But I don't want Mother and him thinking they're going to make my wedding into a big religious event.

She said, "He wanted to know what church Solly was baptised in. Not that it matters, in the eyes of God. He was just curious."

This is the first time I realized I hadn't told them. Danger: subconscious at work.

I said, "We want Father Phillips to perform the ceremony."

"He does such a beautiful job. We just saw one last month, the Andersons. Do you remember Julia Anderson? She went to your high school. She's a couple of years younger than you."

A Louise Pennybaker classic. Just in case I should ever forget how old I am, even if I am FINALLY getting married.

She said, "But anyway, dear, what church was he baptised in?"

I said she must have a suspicion. She said, "Considering his Spanish name, I would guess that he's Roman Catholic." She looked at me like she was pretty sure she was right. "There's nothing wrong with that. We all read the same part of the Bible."

But she was holding her lip with her teeth, which is how she prepares for a big disappointment. However, she was showing that she was willing to bear the pain. Like our Savior. To save mankind. To see her daughter married. Another miracle.

"Solly wasn't baptised," I said. "He's Jewish."

Dad ducked behind his newspaper. The room was silent, like we were all dead. The clock on the wall was making the most noise, and it doesn't even tick. Mom turned her back to me and filled the kettle. Probably several times.

Then she turned back to me. Dad peeked at her. With her chin sticking out to show how brave she was, she said, "Well, so was Jesus."

That was the end of it, at least for today. More to come, I'm sure.

10—45 REPORT

Preliminary Investigation and Interviews of BFI
Job Number 62—4013

Incident location: 348 Broadwell Ave.
Incident date: June 14
Incident time: 12:10 PM
Names of victims: Three/unknown
Nature of injuries: Burned beyond recognition
Bodies removed to: County morgue
Cause of incident: Incendiary
Smoke detector present
Synopsis: The bodies show deep and thorough
burning. Identity of one can be surmised from
location of finding. However, all require
corroboration by laboratory methods.
DOA desk physician: E. Borakove

IT ALL STARTED with Roots. God, that's almost twenty years ago. (I can barely see the change in myself, but how the leaves have fallen around me!) People flood into my library to chart their family trees. I am pleased when they walk out after weeks of tedious work feeling that they know more about themselves. Not that I'm convinced that they do know more. It is true that they are now aware of many new dead people, but what more can you know about yourself knowing about them? I do believe that the illusion of self-knowledge is real; if a custodian finds that his great-great-uncle was a duke, he puffs out his chest just a bit as he buffs the floor.

Part of the problem is what the genealogists look for. It's not the gritty brown of their ancestors' lives. It's only how they were better than others' ancestors. I nudge my scholars to start with the fact that the smartest, richest, bravest, and most beautiful of men has two arms, two legs, two eyes, laughs occasionally, thinks most of the time about himself, grows slack with age, and on and on. I try to make them go beyond the beginnings of their families or their ethnic groups, to the common trunk of human experience. Few do.

Sean O'Reilly. He was consumed by an ancestor's role in one of the innumerable power bloodbaths in medieval Ireland. I wanted to know other things: how often he washed and changed his clothes. How did he and his wife manage to have eleven children in a one-room hut, and why didn't the children become psychopaths like Freud's Wolf Man from watching their parents procreate? (Or did they?) How did the wife manage with all her children, without running water? How did they meet the great daily demand for food? How on earth did she endure her undoubtedly constant vaginal yeast infection? Did she give two hoots about her husband's politics (but did she pretend to?). Did he ever help around the hut?

Why am I writing all this? It's got to be Solomon's suggestion that I look into our family history. I suppose I did mention it to him some time back. I feel a tickling of curiosity, and I'm not sure what to make of it. Maybe he's right, it's because the Beneviste name is about to pass on to another generation. I hope I don't become another victim of historical vanity.

THERE WAS NO possible way out. It was time to bring Solly home to dinner. A year and a half of careful scheduling had to end sometime.

Jeffrey was there, even though I asked Mother not to invite him. He must have figured this was too good to pass up. I saw trouble in his eyes. But if I begged him to be human I would have made it even worse.

He jumped up and pumped Solly's hand. "You sneaky Hebrew. If I had only known I would have offered you some work. I've been looking for a Jewish accountant."

We were taking the express train to hell.

Solly said, "Sure, just as long as you know we're a lot more expensive than gentile accountants."

Jeffrey laughed.

Mother said, "Solomon, rest assured that your relationship with God is none of our business. We're just so happy you're going to join our family." I believed her. I just wished she would stop right there.

23

Jeffrey said, "I always wondered how a Hispanic guy could be so clever. You don't think of them as clever, do you? You think of them as passionate and foolish, you know, running with the bulls. And sleeping a lot. The siesta culture."

Father had already poured everyone a drink. The family gets nervous without one in hand. Solly asked for a martini. Not good.

Jeffrey would not let go. "All this time we're hearing about a guy with this Spanish last name and all this education. I couldn't figure out exactly what you were."

I said to Jeffrey, "Someday I hope to figure out exactly what you are."

Mother said, "All right, children." Like we were in kindergarten.

Jeffrey said, "I think it's great we're getting some Jewish blood in the family. We're too vanilla. It will certainly boost the IQ of Allison's children. Must have been a whopper of a dowry, huh Dad?"

Dad put his hand on Jeffrey's shoulder. That bought a few minutes of peace.

We started dinner, but I could barely eat. Now it was Mother's turn. "So, Solomon," she said. Casual as an air-raid siren. "It is exciting for us to welcome someone from a different faith to the family. It reminds us how wide this world really is."

Solly nodded. I was wishing an airplane would crash into the house.

Mother said, "I once knew a rabbi. A very devout man. I admired him very much."

"What did you admire about him?" asked Jeffrey.

"He was very admirable. You just had to look at him to see it."

Jeffrey said, "You mean because of his Pope's hat?"

Mother said, "It was lovely red velvet with gold embroidery. He was short, so I could see writing on it. That was probably in Yiddish?"

"Hebrew," said Solly.

Jeffrey said, "So you admired his red velvet hat?"

Mother said, "You are intentionally missing the point."

Jeffrey said, "That was very stimulating, Mother. Sol, now you tell her about a deadly dull Episcopalian priest you know."

"Oh, hush," Mother said. "I just wanted to know, Sol, why you don't wear a yommaka."

Solly said, "I'm not devout at all. I had no religious training."

Jeffrey said, "What did you think? They all wear them?"

Mother said, "I wasn't sure. I'm new to this."

Jeffrey said, "No, Mother. They're all over the place. You can never be sure. They can be at the grocery or the post office, or even at the DAIRY QUEEN!" He said that so loud that we all jumped.

Then no one spoke, and that was even worse. Finally Solly said, "It's fine, Mrs. Pennybaker. Is there anything else you'd like to know?"

"I hope you don't find me rude," Mother said.

"Not at all."

"Good," she said. She brightened. "You'll have to meet Father Phillips. He's looking forward to meeting you."

Jeffrey made like he was tightening a screw on Solly's thumb.

It didn't get any better all night. Something like this was going to happen sooner or later, and better in Mother's kitchen than at

the wedding, in front of Mrs. Beneviste. If she and Mother somehow never meet that would be fine with me.

Solly drove me home, but he didn't stay. I couldn't blame him.
Still, it's the first time he ever passed up a chance to be with me.
I don't want him to make it a habit.

I TOOK AARON'S family Bible down from the shelf tonight for the first time since he died, all these long, long years ago. It made me cry. The sweat stains along the spine made me think of him sitting in the overstuffed chair, his large, gentle hands cradling the book, his head down, his hair falling into his face. He was no more devout than I am, but he loved the stories. His parents, unlike mine, didn't poison the Bible for him in the name of assimilation. Assimilation! As if the world hasn't eternally dishonored that daft concept.

I had no idea that it was published in 1689! What exquisite care the Benevistes have shown! The opening pages, left blank for the family history, have been carefully filled in by each generation. My Solomon is the last name, recorded in Aaron's elegant script. (The entire family were wonderful draftsmen.) I see that the first Beneviste to reach America, in 1690—at Newport, Rhode Island of all places—was a young man named Solomon, with his bride, Miriam. That's nice. I wonder if I knew this in my youth and forgot, or if I was guided by a mystical hand when I named my son.

Except for the last two generations—people I met—I know almost nothing about the family. I remember asking Aaron to tell me, and he said that there was no rush, that our dotage would be devoted to family tales. He promised to buy us matching rockers. He promised.

Most of the Benevistes in America have been merchants, and all have stayed in the northeast except for a few in Georgia and New Orleans. We have had an occasional soldier (Revolutionary War, Civil War (proper side), and World War II), banker, teacher, and even some farmers early on.

What will Solomon, Allison, and the next generation make of this? How many millions of families, of all faiths, have the identical profile?

There I go, just like the others. Only interested in the family Prometheus.

A piece of tissue paper slipped out from between the pages. I immediately recognized the handwriting of my Aaron. He had drawn my little bud on our tree. What a dear! As if he knew that someday I would be sitting here doing this without him.

But what he wrote stunned me. According to Aaron, our great-grandfathers were brothers, sons of Moses Beneviste (father of twelve children by three wives). This means that Aaron and I were third cousins. Third cousins!

I must have confused my grandfather Moses with the older Moses (I never met either). I always thought that Aaron and I were first cousins, our union absolutely enjoined by law of God and man. From our first flirtation until the day of the wedding I lived in terror of the discovery of this fact. (How could I have been so ridiculous to think that no one in the family would notice?) At the ceremony I felt the sweat of sin rise on my back; I turned so that when Aaron kissed me he wouldn't plant his hand there and make the wet show. I knew that such a marriage was very wrong. But I loved him so deeply that I stayed with him even so. Maybe this is why I avoided the Bible all those years.

Another sensation from twenty-five years ago: sitting in the emergency room as Aaron died, my grief muted—people thought I was cold!—because I felt that our incestuous violation had finally been answered.

And today I find that he died for no reason at all! No. I mean that there was no violation of natural law involved. Did I ever really believe there was a reason for his death? I'm starting to sound positively superstitious. Still, today's news makes his death seem like another anonymous point on a mortality curve, rather than the work of God's angry lash. I don't know if I could have endured it if I thought about it this way then. I insisted on it being much more. Can I give that up?

27

I RETURNED TO the scene of the crime. Mother didn't have much to say, which was a great relief. I was expecting all kinds of fallout about the dinner. She scrubbed the kitchen table until it was absolutely spotless and then brought out the new Gospels. Yes, the bridal magazines, each one of them thicker than the phone book. She opened the first page she clipped and said, "That's lovely. How about that one, dear?"

The model looked like a six-foot tall wedding cake. You almost expected to see little bride and groom dolls sitting on her head. Her skin was perfect and bronze, not fish-belly white, like mine. Her hair was jet black, not Pennybaker mousy, so of course it looked great against the white lace. The worst part was that the whole dress looked like it was held up with her boobs. Which means that it would pool around my ankles. It was hard for me to imagine what my dear mother was thinking.

She said, "How about this one, dear. My, how beautiful she looks!"

I said, "Exactly. That's how beautiful SHE looks. Remember how I'm built, OK?"

"You have a lovely figure."

Since Louise's wedding, when she was pretty foxy, she's grown an immense cow chest and belly. It's been decades since she worried about filling a cup. I said, "I'm slender, Mom. I can't fill out the front of a dress like that."

"Nonsense. You simply have to watch your posture."

"Anyway, I don't want one of those gowns off the shoulder. I'd spend my wedding worrying that it was going to fall down. And those big puffy sleeves. Please! It's the return of Bridal Barbie."

She was genuinely surprised. I flipped through the magazine and showed her a few. I said, "First of all, I don't want it to be really really white."

"Why? Don't you qualify?" I can't believe she said this. I ducked it.

I said it was too bright. I want a soft color, maybe an off-white. She thought for a minute, then she gave in. I was surprised. I don't expect many victories about the wedding. She said, "As long as it looks like it's supposed to be white."

I showed her a gown on a model built like me. It showed a little shoulder, but emphasized a long, slim torso, and looked like it would fit and stay put. It had a fake-out plunging neckline that started plunging around the Adam's apple. It didn't show anything. Perfect.

She said, "But it's so plain. How can you be a bride without lace?"

"It's a beautiful taffeta. The skirt is nice and bouffy. Very wedding-y." I don't want to feel like I'm being married in a big doily.

"But it's your wedding gown!"

"And there's also a veil, and I'll have a garland. It won't be at all plain. Really!" I was almost pleading.

I could see she was restraining herself, and I appreciated it. She said, "What do you have in mind for bridesmaids' gowns?"

I chose dresses that wouldn't be too expensive and wouldn't take endless fittings. However, I should make Trudy buy a dress like the one she made me buy. Let her spend $550 and five fittings to look like a peach yogurt cone. Anyway, I chose dresses with fitted bodices, a dropped waist, a skirt that's slightly puffy but not too much, and plain cap sleeves. My bridesmaids will actually look like people. They might even wear the dresses again. I found a picture in one of the magazines that was pretty close to what I had in mind.

"What color?" Mom asked.

"I'm not sure. Pastel something. Do you know what you're wearing?"

"I'll follow whatever you choose. And so will your mother-in-law-to-be."

I hadn't even thought about her. God! Whatever I wear, she'll blow me away. Best not to think about it.

I said, "We don't know what Mrs. Beneviste is going to wear."

"No we don't. But she said that whatever we decide, she would plan accordingly."

"She said? When did she say?"

"When I called her on the phone yesterday."

"You didn't!" I put my hand over my mouth and pinched my lips closed. Otherwise I would have screamed.

29

She said, "What's wrong with you?"

She had no right! She probably embarrassed me in a hundred ways she didn't even realize, in addition to those two hundred intentional ways. But what could I say to her? That I was ashamed of her? And now I was ashamed for feeling that way. I said I could have introduced them. She said she was eager to speak with her, and she thought I would be pleased. Of course now I had to ask what they talked about.

"We spoke about her son, and my daughter, and their wedding. Are you feeling all right?"

"You didn't get into the religious thing, did you?"

"I told her about our church and Father Phillips, and how happy we are to have them. What are you worried about, that I tried to convert her?"

The mere thought made the room wobble. Mother carrying the banner of the Ladies Auxiliary of the Church of the Ascension to Miriam Beneviste. The bloodiest day for the forces of Christ since Ben Hur times.

Mother laughed. "You told me how tough she is. I found her to be very agreeable."

"Look, this is my wedding, and I want you to leave Mrs. Beneviste to me. OK? I mean it."

How demented was that?

INTERVIEW SHEET

Complaint—Follow up Information
Interviews of BFI Job Number 62—4013
Investigator: C. Hirschon

1. Interview with Father Phillips, priest of
Church of the Ascension. He stated that wedding was
planned for June 14, day of fire, between Solomon
Beneviste and Allison Pennybaker.
2. He stated that several hundred guests appeared
at the church on said date. Solomon Beneviste,
Miriam Beneviste (groom's mother), and Allison
Pennybaker did not appear.

I HAVE WAITED a week to record this and leave it behind me. It's absurd to suffer for passionate decisions made honorably thirty years ago. I married my (I thought) first cousin because I loved him. I adored him. That was all.

Yes, the thrill of conspiracy followed me until the final night of our marriage. (I thought Aaron never discussed it with me because he too was deeply ashamed; now I realize he never even suspected.) Yes, it was exciting to stand under the *chuppa* and think that my untouched body was being given away in (inadvertent) sin. Yes, it was deliciously exciting to know that every night we were defying five thousand years of the law of civilization.

Still, I did it only because I loved him. The rest was serendipity. I hope that by putting this on paper that I free myself of these terrible thoughts.

Louise Pennybaker called. She was clearly nervous. She kept telling me that Solomon and Allison make such a handsome couple. I would never flaunt Solomon's beauty, as it cannot be denied. If she is trying to convince me of Allison's presentableness, she needn't. Allison's looks, like the rest of her, are growing nicely on me.

I asked her if she knew that thoughts of marriage had been in the air. She said the announcement was quite without warning (a wonderful way to put it). She hastened to add that they were so pleased Allison was with someone like Solomon. I should have interjected a platitude right here, but I was slow, and she began to chatter: she had been worried that Allison would never get married at all, that she would never land a man of quality, and so on. I didn't say a word. I was embarrassed.

Then she told me something extraordinary: she is a licensed chalice bearer of the Episcopal Church. I know that she was trying to impress me, or perhaps to assure me that I would be in good hands inside the church. But I found myself considering a crime I had never imagined: chalice-bearing without a license. I visualized a leather-clad minister on a motorcycle roaring up the steps of the church, reaching the altar just in time to save someone's lips from the touch of an unsanctioned cup.

I lost track of the conversation during this rumination, and I believe that my silence was taken as assent to Louise's proposals. So be it. I guess I don't much care if her church is the launch of the marriage, so long as the direction is toward the right God—a union in true, passionate, life-long love.

BAD NEWS. I spent the afternoon making some calls. Peter kept walking by my desk and giving me weird looks. I haven't told him about the wedding yet. He's just the kind of guy who would flex his middle management muscles and refuse to give me time off for the honeymoon when I want it. But I have to tell him before somebody else does. That would really make him mad. Remember to do this.

Anyway, I figure we can't have less than 175 people without hurting anyone's feelings, and this is what it costs:

First hor d'erves (or however you spell that) passed around on trays. Then a dinner of chicken breasts and rice and vegetables (the cheapest dinner they had). The cost: $35 per person. That's $6125! Plus about $1000 for the help. I never knew this would be so expensive.

Then for the bar (there's no way out of that): $600 for three cases of acceptable champagne, $700 for hard liquor, and $200 for beer and mixers. That's another $1500!

Throw in $600 for the band, $350 for the cake, $800 for the flowers and floral arrangements, $750 for the hall, and $200 for the minister. That doesn't even count the dress, and the one I really want costs $1800! And you know things are going to pop up at the last minute. Like the photographer. That will cost a fortune. Getting married is a disaster!

Solly and I can't afford this. I know Mother and Dad are going to pay, but I don't want to ruin them. Maybe we should go to town hall. I know Solly would be just as happy. Mother and Dad might not like it, but it would be better for them in the long run.

Now it's later. This is what Mother said about the money. "We'll do everything we can to help, dear."

I said, "What do you mean—help?"

"I mean we'll do the best we can. I think this wedding is going to be wonderful."

"Mother, it's going to cost more than fifteen thousand dollars! Can you afford that?"

"No, of course not. But as I said, we'll certainly help out."

"You can't afford it? I can't believe this. Why didn't you tell me?"

"You had other things on your mind."

"Not any more."

She said, "Calm yourself."

"How can I be calm? I don't get this. Didn't you think I was ever getting married? Am I that gruesome?"

"Of course I knew you would get married. It was just a matter of time."

"Then why didn't you put anything aside?"

"We are not wealthy, Allison. I shouldn't have to tell you that. Be realistic. Things might have worked out better if this happened before your father retired."

Mother still didn't get it. I said, "Well, we're going to have a very small wedding, or it's going to be something informal, like a big picnic."

"Fine." Fine? Then she said, "What does Solomon have to say about this?"

"The wedding is the bride's responsibility."

"Isn't that a little bit old-fashioned?"

"Mother, this whole wedding is old-fashioned."

"I think he would be happy to contribute. Wouldn't you if you were in his shoes?"

"His shoes?"

"Yes. Sturdy accountant shoes."

"Mother, he just started his own firm last year. He isn't making much yet. It will be years."

She gave me that "don't tell it to your mother, who has been around the block a few times" look. What is she thinking? THEY always have money? No. Not Louise. Even she is too enlightened for that.

She has never let me down like this before, and it hurts. I have to talk to Solly. Why is the thought of that making me feel so sick?

I TURNED Aaron's Bible upside down and flipped through the pages, to be sure that no other surprises were lurking. Then I returned to the family history, to the lovely calligraphic signature of Solomon, the first Beneviste to reach America. The fine paper is worn down there, as if many of the subsequent owners of this Bible have run their fingers reverently over his name. People don't realize the destructive acids they dispense with their touch.

I think of this fine gentleman as Solomon I. I see that he and my son are by no means the only two by that name in the family tree, yet somehow the others don't fire my interest. I am no scholar. I am a mother. And as a mother my heart turns to 1690. Why in the world would Solomon I want to come to Newport, Rhode Island, into the wilderness, away from the sanity and civilization of Europe? The family Bible tells me nothing more.

36 Answers from the library: Newport, Rhode Island was probably the best choice for a Jew in America. It was a religious sanctuary, founded in 1639 by Roger Williams, who was expelled from the Puritan Massachusetts Bay Colony for requesting that it provide the religious freedom that the Puritans had demanded from England.

I saw a wonderful portrait of the Puritan Poo-Bah Cotton Mather. He was wearing a yarmulke, because to him the Puritans were the real Jews; he labored to demonstrate the failures of the Old Testament. On a literal level the Old Testament is absolutely ridiculous, at least what I know of it. But it is hard to imagine that anyone who lives by the New Testament, surely the silliest book of all, can cast the first stone.

Many of Newport's Jews were merchants, whose sailing boats visited such diverse places as Newfoundland, England, Surinam, Lisbon, the West Indies, and all the American colonies. Some fished and whaled. One Aaron Lopez became the largest shipowner in Newport, which became America's biggest port during the eighteenth century. I saw a plate of a Gilbert Stuart portrait of him. He was a nice looking man.

What did Solomon I and Miriam I do when they arrived? Perhaps he worked for Aaron Lopez, spending his days hunched over a big desk, quill in hand, inventorying the ships coming and going. She raised the children. They were probably economically comfortable—the entire city was, until the British captured and ruined it during the Revolutionary War.

The Jews were said to mix amiably with the Christians of Newport. In their famous synagogue—still standing—George Washington declared that the American government "gives to bigotry no sanction, to persecution no assistance." A good man, that George Washington.

Still, this was the first Beneviste address in America:

> Solomon and Miriam Beneviste
> Jew's Street
> Newport, Rhode Island

WHY DIDN'T I just ask him? What's wrong with me? Instead I told him I was at Mother's looking at pictures of Jeffrey's wedding and the 250 guests. I said I'm glad we're not going to have nearly that many, and he agreed. I said I didn't know how they swung it, since Margaret's parents are retired and don't have much money. Allison, you are so smooth.

He said, "I guess if people want it badly enough they find a way."

Now what was I supposed to say? I want it badly enough, so you find a way? So I changed the subject.

About a half hour later I told him that Mother and I were talking about the wedding plans. And I just happened to mention that she and Dad will help out all they can with the funds. But they don't have very much.

He said, "It's kind of them to offer."

I couldn't stand it. He wasn't even getting angry! I said, "They can't afford it. I'm sorry, Solly. They just can't." I was about to burst into tears.

He was very calm. He said, "What do you think we should do?"

"We could have a smaller wedding, but I don't know."

"My family is little, so it's not an issue to me."

Then I realized he wasn't going to help. Well, why should he? He said, "What do your parents expect you to do?"

"I know Mother would be mortified if everyone who gets invited to every wedding in the family isn't invited to ours. It's a big damn Pennybaker deal. Even if she's not paying for it. Maybe we should elope. We can afford that."

"But you wouldn't like it."

"No. I wouldn't."

Then we didn't speak. And I had one of those realizations that it's better never to have—like you really don't look like a cheerleader, and the problem wasn't favoritism on the part of the judges. I didn't want to admit what I was thinking, but he forced it out of me.

I said, "I want to have a large wedding, with all my family and friends. I really do. I've always wanted that. I'm sorry. Do you hate me?"

He said, "Not at all. I think it's sweet. What do you want from me?"

"A little concern, maybe. It may be my silly dream, but it's your wedding too."

"No, I mean how much money."

I couldn't believe he said that. Still can't. Or that I thought he wasn't going to help me. I said, "You mean, you'll come up with fifteen grand?" Yet more smoothness.

"Don't thank me, not yet. I'm going to have to talk to the bank."

"Who would give you a loan for this?"

"The Beneviste Bank. No one else would accept the collateral."

Miriam! Here I am trying to ease Solly from her manicured hands, and now we're pushing the whole thing right back into them. We'll go ahead and ask her, because we really have no choice. But I know it's a big mistake.

I TOLD SOLOMON what I had found about the family in Newport. He was at best politely interested. He said—You always told me that family histories are as much myth as fact. You make of them what you like. I'm your son. Isn't that enough of a history for me?

—I'd like to put these people someplace. A specific job, a specific home. A portrait. Something to bring them more to life.

He said—What did you find in the safety deposit box?

I had never heard of a safety deposit box. He said that Aaron opened it, and that I was probably still paying for it from my savings account—which I never noticed.

The thought of it kept me up most of the night. What could be in it? Immunization documents, marriage records, military records, financial information. What else? Photographs? Deeds, locks of hair, worn wedding rings? Could Aaron have hidden things from me, like love letters from another woman? Impossible. So why is the news of this box so upsetting? Why am I having tea at 5:20 a.m.?

Solomon was waiting at the bank at 9 a.m., which surprised me, since he has been so indifferent to my project. (I keep forgetting that my true project is to keep out of the way of the wedding, and he is most eager to help me with that.) I brought the old keys from Aaron's desk drawer, and one of them fit the safety deposit box. Something told me not to throw them away.

Solomon pulled out a document, then another, then a few letters, then a few more documents. They got older and more yellow, the bottom-most ones shedding small bits. I was embarrassed at how anxious and excited I was. Some were written in a Semitic alphabet. I will have them translated. After we looked through the stack I asked Solomon if he was disappointed. I couldn't read his reaction.

He said—Not at all, Mama. This is what I expected.

This is what he expected, yet he wasn't interested. I said— Then why did you come today?

To talk with me. Here. I didn't want to talk. I was eager to
dig into my booty.

He said—It's about the wedding. Here we are with all the
family things, and the wedding is another family thing.

—You can do better than that.

—All right. Allison got some estimates on the wedding and
we can't afford it. And that's without any extravagances. It's
the damned size of the thing.

—No wonder you wanted to talk in a bank vault.

He was pacing around the little room, turning every other
step—What it comes down to is that I need to borrow some
money.

—Borrow?

—Yes, borrow. Of course, borrow. I would never ask you to
pay for my wedding.

—What do the Pennybakers have to say about this?

—They're contributing all they can. I don't know how
much.

—You're satisfied with that?

—They're honest people.

—What were they planning to do if you could not provide
this money? I assume the large affair is their idea.

—I don't know, Mama. I don't mind. What's money for?

A good tack for him. I said—So when could I expect to see
the repayment of this loan?

—What day? God! What day do you want it? I'll sign in
blood.

—Do you think I should extract it when you are buying
your first home, or having your first child, or saving for his
college? When would be a good time?

—Somewhere in there.

—And what is the security for this loan?

—Security? I never thought about that. How about my love?

I had to laugh—So let me get this straight. You are asking
me for a loan of thousands of dollars that I would be a fool
to expect to see again to underwrite a wedding in a church
whose planning I am expressly excluded from. Is that right?

—Gee, Mama, you certainly have a way with words . . .
—Fine. You should have said so in the first place.

AFTER THE PROPOSAL you walk on clouds. It's like you're the Green Lantern and your ring levitates you up over all the crap in your life. People were telling me to look out, because you come down. The time before the wedding is the roughest of all. I thought sure, sure. But now I'm a believer.

First it was Peter. I still haven't told him. I don't want him to take that on-line marketing project away from me and give it to Grace. She couldn't sell a bottle of calamine lotion to a mosquito farm. But I just know he would tell me that he would be worried that my concentration won't be on my job (which it won't). And then I'll get pregnant, and he can't sit around and wait for my reproductive ambitions to be realized. Those are his words. I heard him say that to Debbie. Obnoxious. Two problems. I already told Susan. She's pretty cool, but you never know. And there's the ring. Every time he walks by I have to put my hands in my lap, or stick them into some pile of papers. I have to do something about this. Tomorrow. I am resolved.

Then Solly. He came in with a big bunch of flowers and said that the weight has lifted. I didn't know what he was talking about.

He said, "The weight that had you crawling around the room only yesterday. The wedding. Paying for the wedding!"

"You got a loan?"

"Better!"

"You landed a new account?"

"No, I got the loan. But Mama isn't going to ask us to repay it."

I pictured Mrs. Beneviste as I told her to keep the hell out of my wedding. Then I told her my parents can't pay much, even though they're going to invite most of the guests. Now Mrs. Beneviste is telling me that she wants to pay for the whole thing. What's wrong with this picture? There's got to be more to it. Is she asking for our firstborn? (No, HER firstborn.)

I said, "I want to pay her back. I don't want to take her savings. She's a widow."

Solly put his hand on his hip. "Mama is offering to take this load off our finances, which we would otherwise carry for years. She wouldn't offer if she couldn't afford it, I assure you. Why do you want to turn it down? Why do you want to insult her that way?"

43

Because this gift will have gigantic interest. I can just feel it. But Solly wouldn't understand. I bet he wasn't surprised by her offer. That's why he was so easy about the whole thing.

I really don't want to get married at town hall. I think about our church with all the flowers, and the women in their gowns, and Solly in a tux. It's all so beautiful. But over the whole thing looms Miriam Beneviste.

Am I being fair about this? Why am I so sure she's expecting payback? I realize why. Because Louise would. Louise would expect me to chew her food for her for the next twenty years. I can't dump that on Miriam. Who could be more different than Louise?

After dinner, I already had his shirt off when he said, "Oh my God! I still have the safety deposit key. Mama might need it tomorrow."

I could not convince him to wait until the morning. I even threw him down on the bed and started on him, and that's not my style. But nothing happened. Nothing.

I am afraid of this woman.

INTERVIEW SHEET

Complaint—Follow up Information
Physical Examination of BFI Job Number 62—4013

Examination of the remains of house at 348
Broadwell Avenue disclosed that fire originated
in the basement, in an irregular area measuring
approximately forty square feet. Pattern of
burning indicates a significant amount of
accelerant on floor. Two open gasoline cans, a
one-gallon and a five-gallon, were found on
basement floor. Fire extended up stairways,
through open door. Fire also extended up cavity
of stud walls (no fire blocks) and through heating
ducts.

Two bodies, unknown, were found together, one
atop the other, three and a half feet from the
south floor, four and a half feet from the east
wall. Third body, unknown, at this point
incomplete (pending excavation of house), found
five feet north of the other two.

Handcuffs found hanging in basement, one cuff
locked around water pipe, the other open. Key in
lock.

Door between basement and garage found open.
Door between basement and first floor found open.
Front door found double-locked and chained from
inside. No signs of forced entry.

Light switches in kitchen and living room found

in on position. Jewelry and other valuables
found (making arson cover-up of burglary
unlikely).

ANOTHER RECOLLECTION. After Aaron and I secured a mortgage from this very bank, we left carrying the documents (and a check? probably not). I remember trembling, not only with excitement about our first home, but also from the fear that some bandit on the street would hold us up. What did a lovestruck eighteen-year-old girl (was I ever really eighteen?) know about the value of a stolen check? Or a mortgage agreement. Very silly.

But this very morning I felt just as trembly as I walked out of the bank with my packet of Aaron's documents. And I admonished myself, since my nervous shiftiness alone might induce someone to rob me. (What a disappointed felon that would be!)

I planned to tear into the papers as soon as I got home. But I didn't. I put them on the table and made myself coffee, and sipped as I surveyed the pile. I now understand what my genealogy seekers have been telling me all along—it is a very special feeling when ratty old papers are your ratty old papers. I tingled to the feel of deeds to homes of several of my ancestors who are no more to me than names in Aaron's Bible. I loved the chatty, elegant letters between unknown Benevistes and others going back to the middle of the last century. Somehow these were mine. And Solomon's. That's what I kept thinking each time I picked up a new document. What would it say to him?

I did not read through everything today. I am protracting the pleasure. It is agony.

I'm going to take the Hebrew documents to the synagogue this afternoon. There is a little string of beads which was trapped in between the papers. They don't look valuable, but who knows?

I felt like a bit of a scapegrace walking into Temple Beth-El, where I never go except for bar mitzvahs and funerals. The rabbi was out for the day, but his secretary was able to recognize one of my documents—a *ketubah*. A religious marriage contract. It is signed . . . And then she said two Hebrew names. Something like Har and Yom. Alien sounds. She asked if they are relatives. Who knew? And then the amazing news: In English that's Aaron and Miriam.

When I looked more carefully at the crooked Jewish letters on the *ketubah* I began to remember signing it. I was led through it, stroke by stroke, the morning of our wedding. This event was eclipsed in my memory by the dazzling day and night that followed.

The secretary pointed out something very interesting. There was a much earlier *ketubah* signed with the very same names.

It's funny how little I have thought about my own wedding this week. Compared to this imminent stiff, *goyisch* event, my wedding was simple, intimate, and gay. I would give anything to see a photo of it, of Aaron and me, dressed in our once-in-a-lifetime finery, young (extremely) and slim, and eager. Why did I have to burn them all? I must have been insane with grief.

It was Mama and Papa's apartment. The chuppah was set up in the living room, and every inch was filled with relatives and neighbors. I remember the heat from their packed bodies, they were so close. I don't remember any of the rabbi's prayers. In fact, I don't remember the rabbi. But when Aaron smashed that cup the vibrations from the floorboards raced up my legs. Never in my life had I felt anything like it. When everyone yelled *Mazel tov!* I took it that they were cheering this new sensation. I'm sure I had no success concealing it then. Even now it makes me blush.

There was restraint in the affair, by my parent's design. It hadn't been long that nearly everyone in the neighborhood received news that relatives had been slaughtered like swine by the Nazis. My parents thought that too ebullient an affair would have been disrespectful. They were far wiser than their young daughter, who was foolish enough to object.

When Solomon stopped by I told him about the *ketubah*, and what I remembered about my wedding. He was moved.

I said—Have you ever been to a Jewish wedding?

—Several. They were nice.

—Did you ever consider having one yourself?

—A Jewish wedding in an Episcopal church?

—I didn't realize how attached you were to the Episcopalian wedding.

—Guys don't care about weddings. We go with the flow.

—What if a rabbi flowed into your Episcopalian wedding?

—Mama, you can't bring this up now. It's too late.

—Perhaps what was good for your father and me should warrant some notice from you.

He took my hand—It would be fine with me, Mama. But the Pennybakers are church-going people. They take it seriously.

—And we don't?

—The way I see it, it's more noble, more Jewish to let the Pennybakers do the wedding their way, where they want, because it's important to them. We don't need rituals.

There was something wrong with this argument, but I couldn't find it right away. I said—I still don't see the harm in having a rabbi.

—What's wrong is that it would be for show. The Pennybakers have a genuine feeling about the church. You've never taken me to temple. Not once.

I don't like this, and I'm not exactly sure why. But I will not interfere in his doing what he believes is right. That is the proper way for me to love my son.

49

TONIGHT WAS THE first time we had dinner with Mrs. Beneviste since she offered to pay for the wedding. I was really nervous. What was I supposed to do? Pick up the tab for dinner, at least? Maybe kiss her shoes? (It's the closest I'm ever going to get to the Ferragamo collection.)

I have to say that I like her. She's strong in a quiet way, which I really admire. (If Peter had her style our volume would go up by a quarter.) She is paying for my wedding, and that's an incredible gesture. She doesn't have to say boo. I think she wants me to stick around, and that makes me really happy.

But this was the ultimate. At dinner she pulled out this little box and told me she wanted me to have it. I got really nervous. I wouldn't take it. I asked what it was. Smooth.

Solly said, "Open it. Mama never tells."

"Are you sure?" I said.

"Yes, she's sure," he said. He was excited.

It is the most exquisite strand of pearls I've ever seen. Antique, large, and the luster is incredible. I said I couldn't believe she was giving them to me. She told me to put them on, and they smiled at me, and it was amazing how much alike they looked.

But enough about that. I ran to the ladies' room to the mirror. I hardly recognized myself, because all I could see were these magnificent globes. I looked sophisticated—that's how great they are.

But this was all wrong. These, on top of the cost of the wedding? No way.

"What do you think?" Mrs. Beneviste said at the table.

I was about to tell her why I couldn't keep them, but instead I burst into tears. I'm not sure what that was about. Maybe because no one has ever shown me this kind of generosity—and still I'm afraid of her. She took my head against her chest. I'm telling you, she's built.

She said, "If you're worried about taking them, don't. You are taking my son. After that, this is nothing."

What can I do? Insult the woman? But I don't like it. Not one bit!

I GAVE GREAT-AUNT Esther's pearls to Allison. She made a feeble attempt to decline, but her fingers betrayed her by stretching up toward them like tentacles of a hungry cephalopod. Christian women love pearls, and she will savor them as I never did. To my eye, real gems are compacted by great mountains, tempered by the heat of the inner earth into hard clarity. They are eternal. Pearls are cloudy and ephemeral, the compacted refuse of sea *tref*. New. New Testament gems.

This morning I went to see Rabbi Hertzenberg at Temple Beth-El. He is a nice-looking man, about my age (though he would never know it), a bit portly, vivacious, flirtatious, and self-satisfied. After he complained about never seeing me at services, he gave me a pitch about the temple, the education classes for children and adults, the "wonderful and diverse" congregation. He's a good sell. Finally he handed over the summaries of the documents. He can provide more detail if I need it, but he doubts I will. We'll see. Then he handed back the beads and said—We don't get too many of these.

I said—Are they valuable?

—Well, you'd have to ask at St. Thomas's, on Lincoln Street. Those are rosary beads. There's a cross right here. See it?

I thought I would fall through the floor of the synagogue.

I raced home and pulled down Aaron's Bible. There it was, on the cover, at the bottom, centered and faded. It took the rosaries to make me realize I had seen it, twice, without noticing it. It was the cross. This is a Christian Bible.

I looked back at the inscription of Solomon I. Had it in fact been thinned by adoring fingers? I held the page up to the light. "Solomon" had been written over another first name, incompletely elided. It looked like Juan—it was certainly a shorter name beginning with a J. "Miriam" was written over "Maria."

My ancestor Solomon was in fact Juan. Miriam was Maria. Christian names.

I assumed our family went all the way back to Mount Sinai.

51

Yet the first Benevistes brought rosaries and a Christian Bible to America. They were Christians. My family is Christian.

That means that the American Benevistes, at some point along the line, converted to Judaism. Madness. They must have had an insistent feeling that their lives had gone wrong—perhaps the way transsexuals describe themselves as women trapped in men's bodies. Did the Benevistes feel they were Jews trapped in Christian bodies? I hope so. Because this news is no easier than if someone told me today that all my life I have really been a man.

I shouldn't be upset. There's nothing wrong with being Christian. Three-quarters of a billion people can't be wrong. Anyway, what kind of Jew have I been? Since Aaron died I have been a virtual pagan. What is there to give up?

I called Solomon and said—How would you feel about being Christian?

He laughed—It's just a wedding. I told you it doesn't mean anything more to me.

I said—What would you think if I found out we are Christians?

—You're not joking.

—No.

—I don't know, Mama. Are we?

—We might be. Does that bother you?

He thought for a second—It seems like it should. But I'm not sure. It feels more weird than anything.

My heart nearly broke when he said this—even though he was agreeing with me, and it would certainly set the Pennybaker hearts at ease. I realized that I wanted him to explode with indignation. But why would he? He doesn't know anything about this aspect of his life, and it is my failure.

The Jewish stamp on this family—whatever it is—cannot be erased by a Christian Bible and a string of beads. There has to be much more to the story.

PROPERTY INVOICE

Physical Evidence of BFI Job Number 62—4013
Property clerk's list of property taken from
fatal fire which occurred at 348 Broadwell Ave.
sent to County Lab for analysis:

1 sample of flooring from basement, area of fire
origin
1 sample of ceiling tile from basement, area of
fire origin
1 sample of stairway riser and runner from
basement, area of fire origin
1 control samples for comparison with above
samples
1 gasoline can, 1—gallon
1 gasoline can, 5—gallon
1 pair handcuffs with key

THREE MONTHS FEELS like a long time, but it isn't. Alice waited too long to order her bridesmaid's gown for Bonnie's wedding, so instead of going to the rehearsal dinner she spent the night altering it herself. (And it looked it.) Jennifer didn't book her hall in time. But her invitations were already out. Her brother had to stand outside the hall and wait for guests and give them directions to the place she did get. That was such a dump that it would have been better just to stay outside. I will not let this happen to me.

I already picked my bridesmaids. I was a bridesmaid for Trudy and Bonnie. Steffy isn't exactly the bridesmaid type, but I think any college roommate will be into it. She'll probably remind me about all the losers I used to go out with. Not that she did any better. I just have to keep her from getting high. I can see her breaking up in the middle of the service—and me with her. No, she'll be OK. I'll call Alice first. This time I bet she orders her dress right away. Margaret, Jeffrey's wife, has to be matron of honor. I think she'd be offended if I didn't ask her. That's fine. She's a little older, so she'll keep the others in line. I don't want to worry about them.

I asked Solly who he had in mind for ushers and best man. He said it wouldn't be necessary. He'll handle it by himself. This I'd like to see, him running up and down the aisles, escorting people to their seats, then waiting for himself at the altar and handing himself the ring. He doesn't know the first thing about the ceremony, so I explained.

He said, "These sound like thankless tasks. Who am I supposed to impose on to do this?"

I said, "Well, your best friend is traditionally the best man."

"My mother is my best friend."

If he's going to stand me up at the altar, he can do it without her help.

So I agreed to take care of it. The only guy I can think of is Jeffrey, and danger lurks. He got way out of hand at his own wedding. He swiped a trumpet from the band and climbed onto a table and kept playing, and he doesn't play. It was terrible. Is this a reasonable risk? He likes Solly. And Margaret will be there to keep him in line, though she couldn't do it at their own wedding. Oh well. I'll try to think of it as bonus entertainment.

Solly still seemed bugged, even after my offer. He denied it— like he always does—but then owned up. Then this happened. It was astonishing.

He said, "This is completely unrelated. Mama told me that she thinks we might be Christian."

"Don't make fun of me."

"I'm telling you the truth. She did some research and she found out the family used to be Christian. I know, it's hard to believe."

He was serious. If he said, "Mother found out that we're Martian," I couldn't have been more shocked.

I didn't know how to touch this. I am happy, because it removes this big difference between us. I was never sure what his religion means to him anyway. He doesn't seem to know much about it. He never goes to services.

Still, it can't be easy to switch religion. It's not like changing panties. How would I feel if I woke up Jewish one day? Weird! I cannot imagine what Miriam must be thinking. More than Solly is, that's for certain.

This is what I said. "Is that good or bad?"

"I don't know that it's good or bad. It just is."

"Do you still want to get married?"

"What a question! It's just a religion. You mean much more to me than that."

Later I told Mother. Boy was she interested! I hope that wasn't a mistake.

55

I MAY HAVE been hasty. Among the documents is a 1691 certificate of circumcision of Solomon I's son. (Talk about unnecessary paperwork!) This means that if there was a conversion, it happened just after the Benevistes reached Newport in 1690. Rabbi Hertzenberg noted something even more interesting—it was a dual ceremony. Solomon and his baby were circumcised at the same time. If Solomon I wanted to be seen as a Jew, to do business as a Jew, he could have put on a yarmulke and no one would have known the better. He must have had a powerful reason to go through this painful ritual.

In the library I found this: Jewish women were known to walk around Newport holding rosaries, as they quietly repeated Jewish prayers. Why? Being Jewish in Europe was still (I mean—as always) cause for arrest. This use of the rosaries traveled to America as an old habit.

Here's my first guess: The Benevistes came to the New World to save their skins. Perhaps they had to pretend to be Christian as a temporary expedient. One of the earliest documents, even older than the circumcision certificate, was a baptismal certificate, a proof of the family's Christianity. Would any of us be alive today if not for this fragile piece of paper?

MOTHER ALREADY HAS the catalogs for my trousseau, and for all the supplies for my new household. I wonder if she has secret subscriptions, and has all the back issues in a big box in the attic. She insisted on standing over me while I went through them. She said she is going to spare me mistakes that she made. Which meant that she had to admit she made some. This was a first, and I know it hurt, but she handled it pretty well. She's in a good mood these days.

It's amazing how her taste is so close to mine. (I guess I've taught her well.) For the table setting I chose Century stoneware—simple, elegant, and it looks sturdy. (I plan to have Solly around for a long time.) Mother liked it, but she preferred the bone china with the gold around the rim. It's like her fancy service, which is very nice. But I said no way am I hand-washing dishes. The dishwasher strips the gold and then it looks cheap.

I couldn't decide about the flatware. Mother picked out the Marquis, with a fleur-de-lis on the handle. Very classy. And Country Radiance glassware. It catches light in an amazing way. Trudy has them.

And now I am ready to entertain my first visitors in the new Beneviste salon. Maybe Trudy. No. Peter. And his wife, if he has one (poor woman.) Anyway, I have them sit and say, "Would you care for some wine in Country Radiance crystal? Perhaps some Cabernet? Let me amuse you with tales of its vintage . . ." But I don't know any. Bad idea. Anyway, then we drink together, and someone, probably me, says something witty, and we laugh. But not too loud, because I don't want anyone spilling red wine on the rug. The furniture is new and it's all white. We have a white cat with long hair, and when it keeps its eyes closed you can't see it. Peter is so impressed that he is bursting to offer me a promotion, and would, if this wasn't a social event. I say, "Dinner is served." On the new marble table is the Century stoneware. They admire my restraint in picking something so cool and elegant. Anyone with less confidence—an essential quality in a businesswoman, but of course I don't need to point that out—would have gone for something with gold around the rim. Then Solly comes rushing in. He gives me a rose and kisses me. I know that Peter's wife (poor woman) envies me down to her touched-up roots. I say, "This is Solly, my husband. We've only been married a month. Can you tell?" He laughs and kisses me again, bending me backwards. I know he wants me, but he'll have to wait. So we eat the French cuisine I have whipped up in no time, and Peter and his wife are bowled over. After dinner we bring out the Country Radiance brandy snifters and sit on the white sofas. My husband is very charming. But every now and then he shoots me a look that says, "When are they leaving?" I am too gracious a hostess to hurry them. They obviously want to become friends with so stylish a couple, and who can blame them? Peter volunteers that the evening has changed his feeling about honeymoon vacations, about maternity leave, about everything. We have shown him that businesses must nurture families like ours. Finally they go. In the bathroom I change into the sizzling lingerie I got at my bridal shower. Solly is waiting for me in bed. He has pulled back the cashmere blanket. The top sheet of our Renaissance Garden linens looks like a fresco filled with beautiful Italian-looking people. My head touches down on a gorgeous Madonna and Solly is on me. Oh, my! I think. He is drowning me in kisses! Oh, my! His hands are running over my body! Oh, my! He is taking me. Oh, my! Oh, my!

58

IT TURNS OUT that many of the early Jews in North America were refugees from some political savagery in Latin America. They were not heading here; they ended up this far north only because they had been repeatedly prevented from landing in the Caribbean. My impression:

My Juan and Maria stand at the rail of the creaking galley every day, in all weather. Their hearts soar as they finally reach port, desperate to begin their new lives. However, a rum-breathed sailor, tattooed arms crossed, blocks them at the head of the gangplank: they are forbidden from going ashore. The ship lies at anchor for hours, for days, for weeks. What can Juan and Maria be thinking after their horrific trip to be halted a hundred yards from their haven? Finally the captain announces the inevitable—everyone will have to pay up. Alas, this bribe will not bring them to shore. It will only purchase the dearest water and provisions in the hemisphere, and just enough to reach the next seaside extortionists. Jews are not welcome here or, it will turn out, anywhere else on the Spanish Main.

The ship heads for the next destination, and the next rejection. Juan and Maria spend, who knows, six months on the shabby craft, their spirits diminishing, their health suffering from the diet at sea, their life savings disappearing into the pockets of fat gatekeepers of the tropical ports. The ship turns north. They know that Jews had landed in New Amsterdam more than forty years earlier. The Dutch West India Company, which owned the settlement, ordered mayor Peter Stuyvesant to admit them, but he found a way to drive out the "Christ-killers" (his words). And so it is good fortune that the Benevistes' voyage ended in Newport.

I have to corroborate this, and I just might be able to. I found reference to the International Migration Ship Registry in London, which has ship passenger lists going back to the time of the earliest settlements. God knows how many thousands of people took how many millions of hours putting it together. But bless them.

I phoned London. They promised to get back to me in two days. And now I wait.

This evening the phone rang, and my heart leaped. Early word from London! No. It was Louise Pennybaker.

She was a different woman. Familiar, chummy almost. She said that she thought of me because she was at their church. After she discharged unnamed duties concerning the wedding, she stopped to look around. Sometimes, she says, you get so familiar with a place that you really don't see it any more. Well, it's just beautiful.

I was wondering what this had to do with me. The building is of no consequence, as far as I'm concerned.

She went on: It looks like an English church, but it's American limestone, white, quarried in Indiana. You can rest your head against a column on the hottest day of the summer and it's still cool. It's a sanctuary for the body as well as the spirit. The stained glass windows—one of which her family paid for, generations ago—are absolutely magnificent, and were constructed by a descendant of the artists who made the rose windows in the Notre Dame cathedral. Such a beautiful country, France. Have I been there?

Yes, I said, but more to the point was whether her artisans had ever been there. There was a good five hundred years between the completion of the two churches.

At the risk of sounding conceited—a risk she took—she said that in her opinion the descendants outdid their forebears. She is dying to take me on a tour to show me.

Another thing happened beneath the best rose window since Charlemagne. She picked up the prayer book and found herself, for no reason, reading Psalms. She read this line: "Serve the Lord with fear, and rejoice with trembling." She found it very disturbing.

She said—I know a little rabbi, a very decent man, very devout. When I read that I couldn't help thinking of him. That poor timid man, cowering under that hat, as if it could protect him from the wrath of this angry God. I wanted to hug him and bring him into our church, where God loves all mankind through the person of his son, Jesus Christ.

There is only one possible explanation for this presumption. Solomon must have told Allison, and she told Louise, that we are really a Christian family. Tonight Louise was welcoming me to the fold, where we pity the primitive Hebrew and his vengeful God, where all men love their enemies as they love themselves.

Louise, did you love me as well yesterday, when you thought I was a Jew, as you do now? Will you love me as well tomorrow, if I find out that I am truly a heathen?

MOTHER IS RIGHT. It wouldn't be a bad idea to have a fancy set of gold-rim china. We wouldn't use it often—just for dinner parties or holidays. We can always buy the Century stoneware. But it's hard to imagine when Solly and I would put down that kind of money for dishes we hardly use. So I changed my choice at the registry.

Just so Mother doesn't get the wrong idea, I'm not going to tell her. She won't know until she sees my new dishes in my new house. By that time the whole thing will be MY IDEA.

THE LIST ARRIVED today, every known international voyage coming north into Newport around 1690, and there wasn't a Beneviste on it. Nothing close. Perhaps the registry made a mistake. I'll have to call them back. With the time difference it's too late now. A long night ahead.

It came to me in bed. I was looking for the Miriams and the Solomons. The Benevistes. The Jews.

But my ancestors were Juan and Maria. Catholics. They could have come from anywhere at any time.

Why is this so hard for me to accept, even if it was a matter of expediency rather than faith? (And why am I assuming it was?)

INTERVIEW SHEET

Complaint—Follow up Information
Documentary Evidence of BFI Job Number 62—4013
Investigator: C. Hirschon

1. Examination of homeowner insurance policy of
Miriam Beneviste, 348 Broadwell Avenue.
2. Policy was taken out with Canyon Mutual, Inc.,
in June 1962, signed by Aaron Beneviste.
3. Policy value has not kept up with consumer
price index. Based on property value estimate of
County Property Board, replacement cost of house
(without personal property lost in fire) is
$40,000—$60,000 higher than the limit of the
policy.
4. Remarks: Arson for financial gain of homeowner
can be ruled out.

THOUGH THE documents say nothing about where the Benevistes came to Newport from, they do mention the name of their ship. The *Curaçao*. I called the ship registry in London again, and waited the two dreaded days. The report: there was no such ship. They warned me that their records are made of random finds in attics and cellars, and are definitely incomplete. That did not help.

I have lost the family thread. I feel a terrible hopelessness. What will I tell my son?

Today I started to pack up the documents to return them to the safety deposit box, though I am not at all clear how they will do anyone any more good than they did me. But I couldn't stow them. There's more in here, I know it. I had to call Rabbi Hertzenberg one more time. After he flirted with me—apparently part of his holy obligation—I told him about the *Curaçao*.

He asked me to read him the note he had made about the ship. It says: 'Passage: *Curaçao*.' Then he said that his recollection is that Curaçao was the embarking point, not the name of the vessel.

I always thought Curaçao is like Devil's Island. He disagreed, and suggested it's worth looking into.

I stayed late at the library. Rabbi Hertzenberg was right, Juan and Maria could well have migrated from Curaçao, a port conquered by the Dutch in 1634. The first permanent Jewish settlers came from Amsterdam in 1659, and by the middle of the eighteenth century Curaçao had a larger Jewish population than all of North America! Many of the rabbis and cantors who founded the North American congregations came from this little island. Can this be?

Shipping in the Caribbean at that time was largely a Jewish business. They traded European manufactured goods to the Spanish and English colonies in exchange for coffee, gold, cocoa, and tobacco. (And I had thought of Jewish commerce of that time as barrels of pickled fish traveling between shtetls on ox-carts). The Jews of Curaçao not only owned several hundred ships, they also served as captains and crews. They even armed their ships and did battle with pirates.

This I never imagined. Juan Beneviste, cutlass in hand, facing down the musket fire of one-eyed privateers, leaving them in bloody piles on his deck. No. I assume Juan was like his descendant Solomon, the accountant, and ran his business from the safety of his home port. Which is just as well.

The Mikve Israel synagogue in Curaçao, the western hemisphere's oldest, has comprehensive records back to the seventeenth century. I cannot wait for morning.

The telephone at Mikve Israel was answered by a Mrs. Nieto, who speaks excellent English. (Lucky Papamiento, the Curaçaon national language, is a mixture of Portuguese, Dutch, English, and African tribal languages.) She said that the synagogue does not conduct searches, but it does allow people with suitable credentials to use their archives.

Well, of course I cannot go to Curaçao. Again I felt that I was at the end. I poured out my story, and the poor woman listened patiently. Something in my tale, or in my pathetic voice as I told it, moved her. And—this may be God's hand in my quest—she offered to look over the records for me. She said just be patient. This may take a while.

My patience is eternal, until Solomon's wedding.

I DREAD GOING to see Father Phillips. Is that a sin? I've been in his inner sanctum a couple of times, and I remember it as a near-death experience. Why do I have to discuss my love for Solly and my feelings about my church in a room that smells like it's been buried for a couple of centuries? Maybe he'll show mercy and meet with me in a common room on the ground floor.

Tonight I am showing devotion to Christ. I'm giving up an evening of stroking Solly's tender behind so I can study the catechism. I don't want Father Phillips to even consider making me take those lessons again. That would make me yearn for town hall.

I just read this over. It's a little too rough. I like Father Phillips. He's a nice man caught in a bad office. But it's my wedding, and I don't want trouble. I guess I'm worried about what he will say about Solly. I shouldn't. I'm being unfair.

Catechism question: "What does it mean to be created in the image of God?" Answer: "It means that we are free to make choices: to love, to create, to reason, and to live in harmony with creation and with God."

67

Amen. And Solly's fanny is certainly one of God's finer creations.

NEWS FROM Mrs. Nieto: there were no Benevistes in Mikve Israel or the other Curaçaoan congregation. Nor did she see any in the records of the numerous yeshivas.

This is what I now know. The family was in Curaçao—where they left for Newport—but they were not listed in the comprehensive records as Jewish. The family was Christian, and had been for hundreds of years. There is no other explanation.

I supppose it's good that we are having a church wedding. We have a lot to learn.

Yes, I'm sure Curaçao is a beautiful island, and I would love to accept the invitation of this gracious woman to come visit. Like the ship registry, she warns not to make too much of what she could not find. Curaçao has a far more complex past than most places.

I will write to thank her for her effort. But I'm sure I could never do any better than she has done.

NO COMMON ROOM for me, no. The secretary told me Father Phillips was waiting in his chambers. When he got up from his desk, I was afraid the strain was going to make his eyeballs pop out. He took my hand. His are clammier than ever. It's a wonder he doesn't mildew.

He stroked my cheek. Gross. He said, "My, you've grown into such a young beauty."

Yeah, to an old guy. I sat across from him so he couldn't reach me.

He sat down with a big puff. He said, "How do you feel?"

"Wonderful!"

"Holy matrimony is a blessed state. It gives pleasure even in anticipation."

Something like that.

He said, "On the face of it, marriage can be a troubling concept. How can two adults meld to become of one flesh? You and your betrothed are already complete, independent people."

"We love each other very much."

"I'm sure you do, and that's very important. But the kind of love that young people have for each other, so often based on biological needs, can disappear in time. Marriage must have a more secure foundation than that."

I resolved not to say anything that would make this go on any longer than it had to. I said, "Love is an awfully good start, you've got to admit."

"It certainly would be a terrible trial to be married to someone you did not love. But for a marriage to truly succeed you must always remember where your primary allegiance is."

"I hope you don't mean to my mother."

"I mean to Jesus Christ. The way Our Lord gave himself for his fellow man, so a husband and a wife must give themselves for each other, and lose themselves in pursuit of the other's happiness. The Christian does not marry to be served, but to serve. Not to be made happy, but to make happy. In serving and sacrificing, true happiness is found."

I thought pre-marital counseling meant he was going to tell me

69

not to have sex until after the wedding. I said, "But I'm not as keen on sacrifice as Jesus was."

Again he smiled. Right into his trap. "Jesus is present in everyone. In each of us, hidden to one degree or another, is the man who suffered, died, and was resurrected to lead humanity into the Kingdom of Heaven."

I wanted to hear this as encouragement—Jesus is in me. Instead I felt like he was setting me up to fail. What if I'm not in touch with this? Does that mean the end of my marriage? My failure toward all humans?

And Solly. What is he going to make of this? My spirits were plunging.

I said, "Father Phillips, my fiancé is not Episcopalian. You should know that."

"I know all about it, my child. Your mother told me. That's why I wanted to speak with you alone first."

Mother! "What did she tell you?"

"Don't be alarmed. Only that your Solomon is of the Jewish faith."

"It must be bothering her, if she came running to you."

"No, I wouldn't say that. Perhaps she hasn't seen that Jesus's love encompasses all people, regardless of their creed."

"Jesus's love does. I don't know about Louise's."

He tried to stretch his neck, but it was caught in his collar. He said, "There are a few things you should understand about the Jewish faith that pertain to marriage."

I couldn't believe this.

"I'm sure you know the story of Adam and Eve and the fall from grace. Before God banished them from the Garden, He told Eve that Adam shall rule over her."

I said, "You could hardly blame him, after Eve's stunt."

"The point is that the Old Testament forever gives men dominion over women."

"Does it say that?"

"It's a clear implication of the story."

I said, "I thought that idea came from the New Testament."

"The New Testament says that wives should be subject to their husbands the same way the Church is subject to Christ. But we must keep that passage in proportion. In Christianity all parties are expected to submit to each other. The Christian marriage is a union of equality, the way God originally intended."

"I don't remember hearing this in Sunday school."

"It's there. Trust me. You can only fully appreciate it after a lifetime of study of the scriptures."

So this is how it was going to be. After a lifetime of study Father Phillips found a way around a truly nasty part of the New Testament. And he was going to make relatively benign parts of the Old Testament sound as bad as possible. This was my wedding class.

"According to the ancient Jewish rabbinical teachings a man must not abstain from sexual relations with his wife until he has at least two children. But in our faith marriage is complete when God joins two together. There are no other requirements."

I said, "But who said that a man owns his wife's body?" I remembered this from when I was a kid. It hit a nerve.

"St. Paul said that. He also said that a woman owns her husband's body." Score one for Father Phillips.

"If they own each other's bodies, they are certainly going to have relations. So isn't that pretty much the same as the rabbinical view?"

"But they should do so only because it reflects the glory of Christ."

I had a flash of Solly and me together and naked, and no matter how spiritual I was feeling I don't remember Jesus making an appearance.

Suddenly he started to recite: " 'O prince's daughter! the joints of thy thighs are like jewels, the work of the hands of a cunning workman. Thy navel is like a round goblet, which wanteth not liquor: thy belly is like an heap of wheat set about with lillies. Thy two breasts . . .' And so on."

Wow! I gave up a night with Solly to study the catechism, and now God was rewarding me by making an old guy say this hot stuff.

He said, "That is The Song of Solomon. Jews have a distinctly carnal slant on marriage. That can lead to great disappointment. The Christian marriage is spiritual, which goes on even after the flesh withers."

This was getting ridiculous. Like I would want my marriage to be based on something that only a clammy priest can interpret for me. Like I can't trust my own feelings about the man I love.

He said, "And one more thing. Jesus Christ forbade divorce. Even so, St. Paul specified one case when it is acceptable." He paused. Very dramatic. "The only acceptable divorce is when the spouse is an unbeliever. All through the New Testament the wife of an unbeliever is a model for the scorned, abused Christian who accepted her mistreatment while she devoted her spirit to Jesus Christ."

"I can't believe you're saying this to me, Father Phillips. Do you expect Solomon Beneviste to abuse me because I'm Christian? Is this for real? Is this charitable?"

"My point is that if the husband stays with the wife, as St. Paul says, 'the unbelieving husband is sanctified by the wife.' And your children shall be holy."

I said, "If I sanctify him, why is it all right for him to divorce me?"

"I can tell you from many years of experience that when they reach the altar all people think their marriages will succeed. St. Paul tells us that differences of faith can be too great to overcome. Even by love. That's why we look to Jesus."

"I'm sorry, Father Phillips. This does not sound like the Christianity you taught me."

He folded his hands and said, "Our Lord said, in the Book of John, 'If a man abide not in me, he is cast forth as a branch and is withered: and men gather them and cast them into the fire, and they are burned.' "

So I walked out of my wedding class with my own priest telling me about people like my Solly flaming like marshmallows. What the hell is going on?

I LIKE THE WAY Solomon and Allison are with each other. It's very tender. She obviously prizes him, and he treats her with love and respect. If I can't follow the Benevistes of centuries past through the jungles of Central America, I still have my little family here. Yes.

At dinner tonight Allison looked weary. She told me about the wedding caterer who has trouble speaking English, yet tries to talk them into menus they have never heard of. She says her family would be content with pigs-in-a-blanket, which are cocktail wieners in a blanket of pastry. I like that. Very vivid. She is having trouble collecting the bridesmaids' shoes so she can dye them the same color. It seems that Bonnie has particularly large feet and doesn't want to relinquish the shoes so everyone will see just how big. Solomon said—If everyone can see she has boats, what difference does it make what the number is?

Allison told him he doesn't understand women. The number means everything. Then he said—Then why doesn't she black out the number with a marker?

She looked at me and shook her head. It was the first time I have been taken into confidence by my future daughter-in-law. My, I just wrote the words: daughter-in-law. Not so bad.

She asked me how my family research was coming along. Solomon hasn't asked me about it for some time. I told them about the chase from Newport to Curaçao. I had planned to find the family root before I made my report, but there is no longer reason to wait.

Allison said—I didn't know there were any Jews in South America.

I said to Solomon—Was this what you expected me to find?

—No. But I don't think I had any particular expectation.

—You don't seem to care much.

—It's not that. Since you lost the family line, it has been harder for me to stay involved.

I told them about the Jews who left Algeria in 1658 for Leghorn, Italy. A severe economic depression there sent these desperate people sailing for the wilds of the New World. They

73

landed in Guiana, about as wild as it gets. They were lucky to arrive at all. Many ships were captured by pirates. I said—If you two had been aboard, it would have meant a life of slavery for you, Solomon, and Allison, life in the *seraglio*.

They looked at me blankly. They weren't getting it at all. I could just as well have been telling them about talking mules.

I said—Solomon, can you imagine what it would be like to be forced to leave everything behind and sail off to the jungle, because that is your only chance to survive?

—No, Mama, I can't. And I don't want to.

—What do you think a family history is? An album of old wedding pictures? It is the story of how people just like you endured and prevailed over unbelievable hardship.

Solomon said—I'm sorry, Mama. There is enough misery in the world now for me to go looking back for more. I think the best idea is to try to find the things that redeem life and concentrate on them. For example, I would prefer to think about dessert.

But Allison did not see it this way. She said—What happened in Guiana? Did everyone get devoured by wild animals?

I said—Five years later, when these poor people had just begun to get back on their feet, Guiana was taken by the French. I guess you could call them wild animals.

Allison said—And they took the Jews back to France?

—If only you had been there, Allison. No, the French ordered them all to leave.

She said—For where?

—That wasn't the concern of the French. Just so long as they left.

—That's terrible!

I looked to Solomon—Yes, exactly. They fled to Curaçao, which is where they crossed paths with our family. Before the end of the century they had to flee again, to Venezuela. This time it was an epidemic. Bodies had to be left lying in the street.

Allison's eyes were moist with unhappiness. She has a conscience. She said—That's just awful. I never knew any of this.

I asked Solomon what he thought and he said—No one can be unmoved by such a terrible story, Mama. But I guess I don't feel it has that much to do with me.

Allison said that she, like me, was surprised to hear him say so. I said—Three hundred years is not so long ago. They were not primitive versions of you.

—It's not that. You have been telling us about a group of Jews, and we're not Jews. So what does this have to do with us?

He might as well have slapped me. Just from the scraps I have read, I know these wretched people. I can hear them in their desperate little settlements, laughing in the fields, huddling in fear around their fires, yelling defiance into the night, wondering if anyone is listening. I feel their presence inside of me. And yet they leave my son, my soul, my life, cold as steel.

75

I BOUGHT A pen today and did some serious work on my new signature. That big B in Beneviste has lots of potential. Maybe I'll start it off with a pig-tail flourish like this. Or maybe I'll start on the line and come swooping up, like so. Nothing too grand, though. It has to fit on those little strips of tape on the back of my credit cards.

I got to thinking about Mrs. Beneviste and her search for the roots of the family. Soon to be my family. I'm not sure what she's after. She has already tracked it back hundreds of years. How far until she's happy, the Garden of Eden? She said to Solly: "What do you think a family history is, an album of old wedding pictures?" Well, that is what I thought a family history was. At least that's as much as I know about my family. In our house, if you're a member in good standing of the Highland Club, you have a WASP pedigree, and what more do you need to know? It's an awful thing to say. But isn't it true? Not that it makes us any better. God knows.

I wonder where we were before we got on the Mayflower (did we?). I hate to think we had anything to do with the atrocities Mrs. Beneviste was talking about the other night. It sounds like the worst of it was in Spain and its colonies. I'm almost sure we're from England, where everyone is polite, not hot-blooded like those Spanish. I stopped at home after work to ask Mother.

She said, "Is it you who wants to know, or Miriam Beneviste?"

"Well, I'm proud of our family, and I don't care who hears."

"Great, Mother. You don't have to raise your voice. I'm the only one in the house."

"I'm afraid I can't tell you much about the Pennybakers. Your father's family is hither, thither, and yon. I don't even think of them as a family. Just a group of people with the same last name who try their best to forget about each other."

"What about Uncle Bob and Auntie Joy?"

"An exception. On the other hand, my family, the Rogers, has stuck together. They settled here five generations ago. They're the ones who bought the stained glass window for the church. That was quite a generous act for settlers who came here with nothing. If I was getting married these days, I would have kept the Rogers name. It certainly describes you and me and your brother a lot better than Pennybaker."

"How does it describe us?"

"We're from that line. We're like them. What does Pennybaker mean, anyway? That you bake pennies?"

I said, "What does Rogers mean? That you're pirates? Jolly Rogers?"

"Don't be fresh, young lady. The Rogers family in this country goes back to 1830. That's over a hundred and fifty years."

"Is that all? I thought we came over on the Mayflower."

"Is that all? Your husband's family can only wish they've been here anything near that long."

I cannot believe she said this. I don't know what her problem is, but I will not let her do this to me. So I laid it on her. "Mother, the Benevistes have been here since 1690."

And she laughed! Mother laughed! "Don't be ridiculous."

"They landed in Newport, Rhode Island in 1690. Mrs.. Beneviste has papers to prove it."

"I don't believe it. Anyone who knows anything about history will tell you that's ridiculous."

"How can you say that? You don't know anything about it."

"Let's just say that some things are common knowledge."

"Because they're Jewish?"

"It isn't clear exactly what they are. But all right."

"There were Jews here way before 1830, Mother."

"Or so she tells you. And shows you papers."

"Why would she lie about something like that?"

"To be included. Who wants to be called an immigrant?"

"We're all immigrants."

"After enough time passes, you're no longer an immigrant. We are not immigrants."

This was so revolting that I could have stormed out right then. But I didn't want to go until I had the story. I said, "That's very enlightened, Mother. Let's get back to the Rogers family. What did they do?"

"The first American Rogers were important officials of the King of England. They would sail back and forth between here and

England. Eventually they decided to stay because they were spending so much of their time at sea. I remember my grandmother telling me stories about them when I was a girl. There were times during terrible storms when they would take over command of the ships and lash themselves to the mast so they wouldn't be washed overboard. I'll never forget those stories."

"Do we have any pictures or anything?"

She said, "You mean documents? Like the ones Miriam Beneviste has?"

"No, Mother, like the kind you have."

"They are not necessary. There is no doubt about us, Allison."

"There's no doubt about them either, Mother."

Add this to list of Things To Do:
1. Find out why Mother is so defensive about the Benevistes, and their being Jewish.
Or, simply,
2. Strangle Mother.

TODAY ANOTHER letter from Mrs. Nieto:

The Jewish community of Curaçao was constantly raising money for ransom for Jews captured by Barbary pirates (who would otherwise sell them into slavery). On one list of contributors she saw the name "Isabella Beneviste." It was crossed out, and another name, a Jewish name, was written over it. She found no other citation of our family on the island, not even in the graveyard.

What does this mean? Mrs. Nieto said there weren't many secret Jews in Curaçao, but there were certain incentives to conceal religious identity. There was a pecking order, and Jews, especially in the beginning, languished toward the bottom; they were not allowed to sleep in the safety of the fortress at night, but were left in the wild.

In other words, if there had been Benevistes on Curaçao—and who would make up this name?—they contributed to saving Jews, and did it under assumed names. They did not want to be known; yet they risked their secret identities in this act of magnanimity.

Is the hand of God reaching down to me again? I was sure the trail had gone cold. I will never be able to find this family in Curaçao if Mrs. Nieto failed, especially if they were being secret—and I'm not quite sure what that means. However, these people had to get to Curaçao at some point. From how many ports could people sail there? It couldn't have been that popular a destination. I will find out. My family will not elude me again.

79

I CANNOT BELIEVE Mother dislikes Jews. We hardly know any. Even so, we're not nearly blue-blooded enough for that. What bothers her is that the Beneviste family was here before ours. She doesn't resent Mrs. White from the church, whose family came over four hundred years ago. That was in a slave ship. The Benevistes probably didn't show up in first class either. Mother should think about that. Maybe it would make her feel better.

I have to write something down about Solly. He is the best lover I've ever had. Being with him is like being filled with helium and floated up over everything bad. I know every second I'm with him that he wants me, ME, and not some generic woman with warm parts. He really loves me. My only fear about getting married is that someday he won't look at me the way he does now, like I'm the only woman alive.

Today I have another thing to worry about. We were together the other night and nothing happened. It was after that dinner with his mother. We got into bed, and nothing happened. It was the first time.

No, it wasn't the first time. The night he returned that safe deposit box key. Wait. There was the time after dinner with my family. He went right home. Well, I can't blame him for that.

God, look at this. I'm making a record of Solly's only failures! If there was enough room in this book I would make a record of hundreds of smashing successes!

Even so, it bothers me when he's not interested in me. I'm saying it here. I wouldn't say it to him. I don't think sex is ever improved by pressure.

It's not just sex. There have been lots of nights, even a couple of years, when I didn't get much of that. It's just that I don't understand what turns him off, and I get afraid he's losing interest in me and he'll leave me. That sounds ridiculous after a couple of nights, but I can't help it.

Maybe it's nerves about getting married. I've heard about guys who lost all interest while they were engaged, even though they were on fire just before. Unfortunately that's not something I can ask Solly about. He would never admit that he wasn't interested.

Or maybe it's this family history stuff. The more his mother tells him, the more he seems to drift away. He won't discuss it with me. Religion makes normal people crazy. I think I'm a good Episcopalian, but I do it in church, the way I'm supposed to. When I go to bed with Solly, I want him to be my savior, and I want my body to be his altar. I think that to honor God properly we should have daily services. And occasional vespers.

JUAN AND MARIA (or your fathers or grandfathers), you came to Curaçao from one of only two places: Amsterdam or Brazil. Amsterdam has always been a lovely and tolerant city, and I am certain that you wouldn't leave it. Why? Because I wouldn't, and I assume you are like me. Is this good methodology? At this point it's probably as good as anything else.

Brazil. This leaps out at me: From 1548 on, many heretics who were convicted by Portuguese tribunals but who were repentant were deported to the vast Portuguese territory of Brazil. Now what exactly is a repentant heretic? Is it like a person who breaks wind and then promises to fix it? Who would believe such repentance? This is very odd.

Holland and its formidable Dutch West India Company were at war with the Spanish and the Portuguese in the New World. In 1630 a Dutch fleet and army, aided by local Jews, took the Brazilian port of Recife, thereby controlling the richest sugar-producing area in the world, and the plum of the Portuguese empire. A few years later the Dutch also conquered Curaçao.

By 1640 there were as many Jews as Christians in Recife. The Dutch, who practiced religious freedom, allowed the repentant heretics to what? pent? They even allowed practice of the tribal religions of black slaves from Africa, and of native Indians.

I called the London registry again, who directed me, naturally enough, to the Dutch West India Company in Amsterdam. They have vast computerized records. Their news: there were three Beneviste males in the employ of the Dutch West India Company in Recife during Dutch rule.

It's wonderful to imagine the Benevistes in Brazil. The women, tan and full-bodied, with long, thick dark hair, run their busy, noisy households. They wear light, colorful blouses and skirts, and walk barefoot on the black soil. The men run the sugar mills and the port, and send their product off to satisfy the sweet tooth of Europe. I see the extended family, and probably most of the Jews, living together in a sprawling neighborhood. These are happy people.

But of course it couldn't last. In 1646 a powerful Portuguese force laid siege to Recife. Portuguese honor must have been a terrible thing, because many Jews, led by their Rabbi Isaac Aboab (the first American rabbi), chose to die in battle, or starve, rather than surrender. I imagine Juan's father and grandfather in the front lines, steadying their muskets as the brass-bellied Portuguese come storming their position. Why did they feel they had to fight to the end? (And bless them for failing.) And the women! What must it have been like when the children wailed from starvation? They must have begged their husbands to allow them to surrender. Rabbi Aboab be damned, their babies were dying! Yet the fight went on.

Finally a Dutch fleet arrived and the city was saved, at least for the moment. The Portuguese continued to raid. Many Jews were driven away, and I wish to God my family had been among them. But they stayed. Perhaps if I had endured the great siege I too would have insisted on remaining to savor the victory. If there had been one.

83

Once the Portuguese had freed themselves from the Spanish yoke in 1640 (the rat freeing itself from the louse?), they formed the Portuguese Brazil Company to contest the Dutch West India Company. But the treasury was depleted. Who would supply the enormous quantity of money necessary to build a great flotilla?

New Christians. What in God's name is a New Christian? Back to the library.

I should have known. New Christians are Jews who converted to Christianity. This cannot be a happy tale, if Jews were willing to die rather than surrender in Recife. After a second siege, Recife fell to the Portuguese in 1654. All Jewish property was seized. The Jewish cemetery was given as a prize to one of the black slaves, who apparently had requested it. May I never know what he had in mind.

The Portuguese were famous for their zeal for putting civilians to the sword. But the gracious, and obviously unqualified, Portuguese commander, allowed everyone time to settle his accounts and depart. Many of the Jews, the smart ones, went to Amsterdam. Others dispersed around the Americas; most New World Jewish colonies were a result of the fall of Recife. Some remained behind to look after their property. They were welcomed to stay, provided they accepted Portuguese religion and rule.

A fateful moment for the family. Aaron and I would have been on the first boat to Amsterdam, but I'm not so sure I can rely on that egotistical principle this time. What path did the Benevistes choose?

YOU CAN GET engaged, wear a ring, tell everyone, argue with your mother. But until you see yourself in that dress holding that corsage, well! Now I believe it.

First we stopped at Madame Reynard's. During all those fittings you worry about what they're doing, because you look like a big baggy pincushion. But today I slid the dress on (slid isn't exactly the word) and it's perfect! It made my cry. Mother wept a little too. I couldn't see the tears, but she did have that tissue rolled up in her hand the way only old ladies know how to do.

Then it was off to Beverly's Beauty salon. Bev said, "Aren't we looking flush this morning. Either you're going for some wedding function, or you got a great big present from the guy this morning."

I slapped her leg. "Not so loud. My mother's right over there."

"Reading *Modern Romance* magazine. I bet she's green with envy of you."

"Why? She's married."

"Exactly."

I laughed so hard we had to wait before she could start on my hair.

Then we drove to the photographer's studio. I like it when the groom is in the wedding photo with the bride. Mother talked me out of it, but I was having second thoughts. There was still time to call Solly. Now Mother had another reason: it's terrible luck for the groom to see the bride in her dress before the wedding. I told her times have changed.

Then she came up with this: "There's something wrong with those men who insist on being seen in the newspaper. People are supposed to look at the bride."

"Nobody looks at the groom?"

"Not in the same way."

"How are you supposed to look at the groom?"

"The groom is important, of course. But the bride is the star. Is Solomon so vain that he thinks the pictures would be worthless without him?"

"No, Mother, he doesn't know anything about it."

"And suppose you split up. What would you do, cut these fabulously expensive pictures in two?"

Split up? Where the hell did this come from? Mother was already counting on my marriage to fail? I couldn't believe it. I didn't know what to say. So I turned my back on her and went into the studio bathroom. It took me twice as long to put on my makeup, I was so angry.

When I came out to get my jewelry and the dress, I pretended she wasn't there. She grabbed my hand. "I didn't say I want you to split up, Allison. Don't put words in my mouth. All I'm saying is that if something goes wrong, this way you'll still have the pictures. Be sensible."

"Get this straight, Mother. We are never going to get divorced. And even if we did I would never want to forget Solly and this moment. And that is why I am going to call him now."

"Don't do this just to spite me, Allison."

"I know this hurts you, Mother, but you have nothing to do with it."

I called him, but he was out. Mother had her way after all.

The photographer's assistants helped me get into the dress. Even with their expert help it took forty-five minutes. I had something old: Mom's silver locket with the picture of Great-grandma Rogers inside. Something new: silk panties. Something borrowed: Trudy's charm bracelet. Something blue: one blue lace garter that Solly gave me!

I came out slowly (not that I had a choice in that dress) and looked in the mirror. With my hair just right, and my makeup, and jewelry. I was the bride. What can I say, I was the star!

The photographer had a whole collection of backdrops. Some were just colors and patterns. Others were locations, like a forest, the top of a mountain, a seaport, in front of a fireplace. He had me on the move for three hours, standing, sitting on chairs, even on different rugs. It was very tiring.

Every time he put me in front of a new backdrop I closed my eyes and imagined that Solly and I were there. First we were hiking in a dark forest. It was cool and damp. There was that sweet woody smell all around. Solly wanted to pull me off the trail, but I was afraid a wild animal would come up while we were in a compromised position. Then what would we do? Flash, flash,

flash. We were at our ski lodge. We just went down the hardest expert trail, breaking the all-time record. Now, as we were relaxing with a hot buttered rum, people kept coming up to congratulate us and ask for autographs. Solly was impatient to be alone with me, but I decided that first we would have an outdoor jacuzzi with a view of the mountain. Flash, flash, flash. The captain of the ocean liner was holding the ship for us. What could I do, Solly wouldn't take no for an answer at the hotel! Good thing I'm the star. Our suite had ocean views on three sides. The captain requested our company at his table, but we wanted to be alone. Solly put on a smoking jacket and popped open the champagne. He had that look in his eyes. Uh-oh! Flash, flash, flash.

Taking off the dress was a shock. It was hard to decide what was real. On the ride home Mother and I didn't talk for a while. That was a relief. I was still traveling around the world with my husband.

Nothing good lasts forever. She said, "What I was trying to say in there is that this is a special moment that you will never have again for the rest of your life."

"Is this about religion? Is this more crap about how we're not going to make it because St. Paul doesn't think so? Because I've had enought of that, Mother."

"This has nothing to do with religion. I don't even know what you're referring to. For once listen to an older woman, who was young once. You are a flower now. That will never happen again, no matter how many times you marry. It's worth preserving in studio photographs. There will be plenty of pictures of you and Solomon at the wedding."

I was ready to explode. I never expected to say this to her, but I did. "Sorry, Mother. I've already been plucked. So I guess the pictures are ruined even without Solly in them."

The rest of the way home she didn't say a word. It's time she respects me as a woman, even if I weren't getting married. I'm twenty-eight years old. I've had my own apartment for five years. I get profit-sharing and I have a 401k.

But after a while I started to feel bad. When we pulled into the driveway I said, "I didn't mean to hurt your feelings, Mom."

"Didn't you?"

"It's time we were honest with each other."

She sighed. She looked kind of sad. "Allison, I expect that you've been sexually active for many years. I preferred to think of you as pure, as I was at my wedding, and as Our Lord Jesus Christ taught we should be. I'm sorry you didn't feel you could allow me the comfort of my illusion."

I came home and I cried. And I'm not sure for who, her or me.

RABBI ISAAC ABOAB returned to Amsterdam after the fall of Recife and became a member of the Dutch rabbinate. He was one of the sixteen rabbis who judged at the excommunication trial of the great Jewish philosopher Baruch Spinoza. This is fascinating. A peer of Descartes, Spinoza insisted on seeing things rationally, mathematically—that was the great achievement of his age. I have always been sympathetic with his claim that God is Nature, and not some egotistical, supernatural being beyond it. Of course he denied the divine origin of the Bible. What reasonable person wouldn't?

Rabbi Aboab must have dreaded the trial. He was not naive; he had read Montaigne, Hobbes, and Machiavelli. Perhaps at some other time he could have dismissed this as normal, youthful rebellion, no threat to this major Jewish community. But not in the age of Portuguese gunboats, and Martin Luther's bloodlust. It was only by heroic adherence to the laws of Moses that the religion had endured thousands of years of God's trials. Spinoza's words threatened to undermine the Jewish determination to continue. So it was said.

How I would have loved to be at the trial! The genius, the passion! If only there were something like it in my time.

How would I have voted? What a question? I understand the need of the rabbinate to preserve the Amsterdam community. But this man was for the ages.

Would I have voted to condemn Socrates or Galileo? Would I have voted to excommunicate Spinoza?

It's 2 a.m. I cannot sleep, and I have to get up at 6:30. It's that damned trial. Now that I put myself up on the judges' bench, I cannot get it out of my mind. After four hundred years, I'm still feeling responsible. Maybe I'm a Jewish mother after all.

Spinoza was in the vanguard of the Enlightenment, which pried open the benighted eyes of the West. He should have been protected and revered. The entire western world had a stake in his work. It still does.

Then what is bothering me?

I keep thinking of Juan and Maria. I've seen them fleeing

to Newport, their fathers fleeing to Curaçao, standing and awaiting their slaughter in Recife. While I feel their fear, I also feel their fortitude, their conviction—their faith.

Faith. That omnipotent, unquestioning direction of life. My family never would have survived without it. This genealogical research has made it very real to me, though I do not share it. Or do I? Am I a secret believer? Is this what is keeping me up tonight? Am I unable to admit it, even to myself, because I live in this unforgiving age of reason? I'm nowhere near ready to take on that one.

Rabbi Aboab had to be a man of true faith. He had watched his God inflict suffering and slaughter on his people during the two sieges of Recife. How could Spinoza, in his cosy home in Amsterdam, possibly understand that kind of blood conviction?

I imagine rabbi Aboab secretly admired Spinoza. Who better to appreciate a genius of the text and the argument than a rabbi. But he understood first the role of faith in preserving his tribe. Genius—am I saying this?—is not the greatest good.

My hand balks. My ink pools on the page.

Here it is. I am not a coward. I commit it to ink: I would have voted with the rabbis to excommunicate Baruch Spinoza.

4 a.m. I'm up yet again. Where is my courage, now that I need it to sleep? Look at the change in my writing. Shaky. Miriam Beneviste has voted to excommunicate Baruch Spinoza, and thereby herself—the head librarian, for a lifetime of service to the rational over the irrational, the enlightened over the mysterious, the individual over the institution. But I will not delete the last entry. I know it belongs here.

When did Jews start excommunicating people, anyway? Isn't that, like wedding arrangements and mixed cocktails, better left to the tribe of the cross?

THIS WAS REALLY bad. At least I think it was. If anyone is reading this, put it down right now. I mean it.

The wedding is only five weeks away. A couple of months ago Solly was part of everything I did. He even came when I shopped for clothes. He sat outside the changing room reading a book waiting to give the thumbs up or down every time I came out. He could never get enough of me. But now! He can get plenty of me, fast. When this started I didn't even write it down, because I was sure it was going to pass. But it hasn't.

I know things get weird before a wedding. Everybody says so. And Solly is such a wonderful guy, I don't want to get all over him about it. I saw Trudy do that to Charles, and it was like watching somebody slowly slide something over the edge of a cliff. But I can't stand it! I finally asked him what was wrong and he said nothing. But, he said, if something was wrong, it wouldn't be anything personal. I said, Nothing personal? How can you get more personal than checking out before a wedding? He wouldn't answer. I wonder if he knows himself.

Our sex life has plunged. I don't know what to do with him these days. I take the initiative—that doesn't work. I play coy—that doesn't work. I get naked—that doesn't work. I wear some of my sexiest night things—that doesn't work. He likes the TV. That's about it.

Last night I decided to keep on my nice work clothes. When we first met he used to undo the side zipper on my skirt and kiss me through the little opening, which is quite an amazing sensation. But he didn't get the hint. He was on the couch and I was standing in front of him, and he was trying to look at the tube around me. That was too much. I reached around his neck and pulled his face into my boobs. I actually put extra perfume right there just in case.

And then it happened. I still can't believe it. He slapped me across the face. Hard. I've never been slapped like that in my life! I ran into the bedroom, bawling. Not because it hurt so much (though it did hurt). Because I was humiliated. The way he turned me down! Am I so horrible that he has to drive me away like a stray dog? My gentle Solly striking me! Never in a million years, I thought!

He rushed in after me. I yelled at him to go away. I rolled myself up and made like I would kick him if he came any closer. And I would have. I didn't want him to touch me, and I didn't want him to see me crying.

He dropped to his knees beside the bed. "I'm sorry, darling. I am so terribly sorry. I didn't mean it." Didn't mean it? "It was a reflex. You feel pain and you swing. You don't even think."

"Well, I am sorry that my body causes you pain."

"You injured my neck. Didn't you know?" This I didn't get at all. "Let me show you."

He pleaded with me to look. He said I know he isn't a violent person. And he isn't.

I had to see if he was making this up. He pulled his collar down, and blood was trickling down the side of his neck. I said, "Oh, my God, Solly. I did that?"

He reached over and tried to take my hand, but I wouldn't let him. He said, "It must have been the bracelet. It felt like you were sticking a dagger in my neck. Not that that's any excuse. But please understand."

I've been wearing Trudy's charm bracelet since the photo session. I ran my fingers over the charms to see if one of them could have gouged him like that. It was the crucifix. It had an edge like a razor. But there was no reason to get into that.

I said, "There's a little golf club charm that's pretty sharp."

"So you see what happened."

I did see. But that didn't mean that he could hit me.

He said he was sorry a hundred times. He was kneeling and bowed his head. I believed him. After all I nearly cut the guy's head off. I said, "If I ever cause you pain again you have to find a kinder way to tell me. You can't do this."

I let him take my hand and he kissed it. "I'll never do it again. I swear it to you."

He sat down next to me and touched my cheek. "I hope I didn't hurt you."

I said, "Let me clean off that cut. You might need stitches."

92

"It can wait."

"The blood is ruining your shirt."

"I have plenty of blood. I have plenty of shirts." He leaned into me. I didn't get it. Then he pushed me over. The good way.

I said, "Don't get blood on my suit!"

He quickly stripped it off me. And he took me, bleeding and everything! He turned out the lights, and I couldn't tell what was blood, what was sweat, what was anything else. As I got turned on, my cheek started to tingle again where he hit me. Allison Pennybaker, girl WASP. I can't believe it! What's going on?

THE INTERNATIONAL Migration Ship Registry records two Benevistes and their families as passengers on the *Vandenburg*, the ship that took Rabbi Aboab to Amsterdam. Thank God. Apparently the other brother was left behind in Recife. I have no way of knowing whether he lived through the second siege.

I just found the answer. Scanning through the national library database, I found the journal of Rabbi Aboab. He refers several times to a Beneviste in his congregation. This man was worried that his brother, Solomon, still in Brazil, didn't appreciate how severely the Portuguese and Spanish were dealing with current (or former) Jews. The rabbi urged the man to get him out of Brazil before it was too late.

Several months later the Brazilian brother wrote that he was converting to Catholicism and changing his name to Juan. (This must be the baptismal document from Aaron's safety deposit box.) The rabbi was fatalistic: once the brother chose to stay in Brazil, a conversion was inevitable. The next mention, several months later, noted that Juan was desperate to leave Brazil. He bought a boat to sail for Curaçao.

I've found him. I know it. This has to be my first American Solomon Beneviste. I will never know what happened to him in Recife, but it must have been dramatic, since neither he nor his son openly resumed Jewish identity, even in Dutch Curaçao. That didn't happen until the grandson, also Juan, landed in Newport in 1690 and undid all of it, changing his name back to Solomon, and correcting the name in my Bible. I imagine that all the Beneviste Juans were Solomons in the privacy of their homes.

One final thing. Juan and his wife, according to the rabbi's notes, were not only man and wife. They were also first cousins. The rabbi mentioned this casually, as if it were a common arrangement. Can there be any doubt that these sensible people are my ancestors?

WE WENT FOR our session with Father Phillips today. But before we did I laid a couple of things to rest. What happened with Solly the other night shouldn't have happened, but it did, and it was as much my fault as his. It was a freak and it will never happen again. Period. At work I finally told Peter about the wedding, and also that I'm taking two weeks vacation right afterwards. Period. If he wants to give my on-line project to Grace, let him. Once he sees what she does, he'll give it right back. Maybe it's time for him to see what I'm worth. Anyway, two weeks isn't so long.

Now Father Phillips. After the hellos, the first thing he said to Solly was, "I understand you are of the Jewish faith."

I said, "Yes." I still don't see what this has to do with our wedding. And it seemed unfair to discuss it in the bowels of a church.

Father Phillips said, "I want to assure you that we welcome you to our church and to our hearts. Jesus loves people of all faiths."

Solomon opened his mouth, but he couldn't think of anything to say. What could he say?

Father Phillips said, "In the early years of the last millenium, there were many marriages between Christian women and non-Christian men. The Church instructed the wives to be reverent both toward their husbands and toward Christ. Allison and I spoke of it last time."

Solly looked at me, and I couldn't think of anything to say.

Father Phillips said, "Now before we start talking about Holy Matrimony, bring me up to speed about your wedding plans. Are you going to have a big crowd?"

"Too big."

"Really? I've seen brides run ragged, but never one who really seemed to mind."

I said, "It's the expense more than the work. It's unbelievable."

Father Phillips said, "Well, here's something interesting. People often think that what goes on at the altar is all that matters in a wedding. That's not so. The meal is also very important. In the book of Revelation, final salvation is symbolized by the wedding of the Lamb and the bride, and the blessed are called to the marriage feast to sit with the Messiah. Tell your parents. It may make the expense a little easier to bear."

"I'll tell Solly. He's paying for everything."

Father Phillips said, "I commend you, young man. That's very generous and good of you." Then he said, " 'If a man would give all the substance of his house for love, it would utterly be contemned.' " And he looked at us like we were supposed to say something. "Don't you recognize that? It's from the Song of Solomon. It follows a line often used in the wedding ceremony: 'Many waters cannot quench love, neither can the floods drown it.' "

Solomon said, "I'm not very familiar with the Bible. But I like that sentiment."

"The Bible tells us about the first marriage, of Adam and Eve, both of them in His image."

I said, "How can they both be in his image?"

"We say that there is neither male nor female, for we are all one in Jesus Christ."

There's an image: Jesus neither male nor female. All smooth. Weird.

"In Genesis God tells man to leave his father and mother and cleave unto his wife, and be one flesh. Now what does this mean, for two to be of one flesh? This is the crux of marriage."

Solly looked at me. The only sense I could make out of this one flesh idea was in bed. But I was trying to think smooth.

Father Phillips said, "When I ask people what they expect in a mate they say someone who is wise, sensitive, understanding, and forgiving, but strong. Someone who is both commanding and pliant, who fulfills their every need. Allison, you're smiling."

"You just described my Solly."

Father Phillips said, "I just described God. No human can fulfill these expectations. The problem is that many people no longer turn to God to meet the needs only He can fulfill. Instead they burden the spouse, who can only fail. Do you know what pollsters found is the primary concern of modern American marriages? The primary concern of the modern American marriage is the modern American marriage. God never told Adam and Eve to count their orgasms or to measure their 'quality time.' It's idolatrous for couples to focus so intently on their relationships, and not about the tasks that God has assigned. Jesus said, 'Take my yoke upon you, and learn of me, and ye shall find rest upon your souls.' In the Old Testament, Solomon, you may know that Psalm 127 says, 'Unless the Lord builds the house, those who build it labor in vain.' Life is work, and marriage helps us do our work. When we forget this, marriage inevitably fails."

Solly said, "We are not afraid of work."

Father Phillips said, "Good. Next time we'll explore the nature of married life. The great Hebrew kings, David and Solomon, had hundreds of wives. You will have to do with one. Unless Allison, like Sarah or Rachel, offers her maid as a second wife."

"Don't even joke about that!" I said. Solly smiled. So did Father Phillips, though I don't think he knew it. Men.

"And we'll speak of sex. The genitals make up only about one per cent of our weight, but in the early days of a marriage command a far greater proportion of time and energy. In time sex will, and should, settle closer to that one per cent level of your life."

I was imagining Solly naked. He is a sight more than one per cent.

"God could have chosen an easier way to perpetuate our species. Yet he chose to do it in a way filled with emotional and spiritual complexity."

As we walked out, I wondered what it would be like if people split like amoebas. Solly said women could pull into a sperm station and say, "Fill it with premium." Horrible!

Sex is complicated and emotional. And important to discuss. Just not with Father Phillips.

ALLISON MISSED our dinner tonight. The invitations, which came back late from the printer, should have gone out yesterday, according to Emily Post. They have to be hand addressed, inner envelope as well as outer, and elaborately stuffed, what with invitation, directions, RSVP card and envelope, and all the little pieces of tissue, lest the others rub. And thus trees die.

Something seemed to be bothering Solomon. His gaze was drifting uneasily. At length he told me he had gone to the wedding class. I had forgotten about this. I imagine I had tried to forget about this.

He said—In the early days, priests told Christian women who married Jewish men to obey them. I was glad to hear it. It means I'll control the TV.

—Why would priests tell women to humor a few Jewish men at the expense of the teachings of Jesus Christ?

He didn't know. He hadn't thought about it that far.

He said—The meal is an important part of Christian rituals. Final salvation happens when the lamb and bride get married.

—Is the lamb's bride also a lamb?

—I'm not sure. Though I must say that I don't see why a wedding between two lambs would be something to celebrate.

Neither do I.

He said—At the feast the blessed come to sit with the Messiah. That's a nice image, sitting around with the Messiah.

—If you have an extra place set for him.

—Christians think that there is neither male or female, for all are one in Jesus Christ.

—Then how is it that there are so many Christians?

—This is because the church tries to see things in a way that will reduce conflict.

—I never thought of male and female as conflicting.

He said—King David and King Solomon had hundreds of wives.

—It's a good thing they lived before Jesus. Or there would have been hundreds of unhappy wives.

—Did you know that the genitals make up only about one

per cent of our weight? But of course they have a much bigger impact on life than that.

I said—Did you know that an atomic bomb the size of a goiter could blow up this city?

—What is that supposed to mean?

I said—It means: What are you talking about? This is a wedding class?

—Don't disrespect these things, Mama, even if you don't agree with them.

He seemed to be inviting me to condemn them. But I would not play into that. I said—I do not disrespect church teachings. It's just that I can't help being suspicious of anyone who says he can prepare you for married life. You will figure it out when you get there.

—What's wrong with some advice?

—You are equipped with everything you need: tolerance, moral sense, and love. And you are marrying a woman who loves you very much.

He looked away from me again. Something has happened between them. Perhaps that was why she didn't come tonight.

I said—Your father and I never had marriage lessons.

—They probably didn't have them then.

—We were terribly young, and we didn't know anything except that we loved each other more than life itself. The night of the wedding was the first time I ever saw a grown man naked.

—Please, Mama.

—I was so scared that I was humming through my nose. That's what your father said. But by the end of the night I knew how to please him, and I knew I could keep pleasing him until the night he died. And I did.

—I'm very happy for you, but don't tell me this.

—You have a moral sense that will guide you. Just like your father. It will never let you down.

—Then we let the issue lie.

—Maybe.

I said—So Allison must be extremely busy.

—When are you going to come to dinner at their home? They've asked three or four times.

I think it might be better to meet at an activity the first time. Solomon said that they will be intimidated by me, and I can control the conversation any way I want. Maybe so. Still I'd rather not. I asked him why this is so important to him. Does he think things between him and Allison would be easier if I met her parents?

He said—We don't need anyone's help. But what's the big deal? We're getting married, and you haven't even met them! They're insulted, and they have every right to be.

This outburst, which drew attention from the next table, soon passed. I will go, and he will be disappointed by the effect. I wish he would just talk to me.

After dessert I said—It is probably going to turn out that the church has been giving us instructions for a long time. Did you ever wonder why the family left Europe, the civilized world, to come here?

—No, I try not to think about things like that.

—Place yourself in their shoes. Why would you leave your home?

He sighed—I don't know. Freedom of worship, economic opportunity? Just like everyone else, I suppose.

—It wasn't like everyone else. We might have been forced to leave. And it might have had something to do with the Inquisition.

He smirked at me—Sure, Mama. Little men in black cloaks breaking people in secret dungeons. And you make fun of Father Phillips!

PETER LEFT A memo on my desk confirming my vacation. Now I'm a little nervous. Maybe I should have asked him if it was a good time to go. I don't know. Would I postpone my honeymoon if Peter asked me? That doesn't seem right. But what if Grace is good at this on-line project? It's not impossible. Then they wouldn't need me. He could leave a pink slip on my desk just as easily. He wouldn't even blink, the lizard. That would be one hell of a way to start a marriage.

So maybe I should have kept my mouth shut when I got home. But I couldn't. I said, "I have to know, Solly. Are you attracted to me anymore?"

"You are the sexiest woman in the world to me."

"You should have said something I could believe."

"But it's true. I wouldn't want to marry you otherwise."

"What do you like about me?"

"Everything."

"Like what?"

"You want a list of what I like about you?"

"That's right. I don't think it's too much for a fiancée to ask. Do you? Do you feel this is an imposition?"

Poor guy. I can't believe I really said this.

He said, "All right. For one thing I love your pale skin."

"I don't believe you. You'd like me better if I had olive skin and black hair, like your mother."

"Anyone can have darker skin, just by lying in the sun. It's common. But no one can have lighter skin. Yours is soft and innocent. It invites my touch."

"But not lately."

"And I love your breasts."

"They're tiny. Unlike your mother's."

"They're firm and beautifully shaped."

"Really? I thought you forgot."

"Nor have I forgotten your profile from behind. The gentle line from your waist to your shoulders. Delicate but strong. I love that."

"But I don't have great hips like your mother."

"I like spending time with you. Even when we aren't doing anything. That's rare."

"But not as often as before."

"You make me laugh."

"Especially when I'm humiliating myself. Like now."

"This may not be the best time to say it, but I feel that you understand me and accept me. That's probably most important of all."

"I don't understand you at all these days."

"You're not going to make this easy, are you."

"I want the truth, Solly."

Truth is there is nothing he can say that will make any difference, until things are normal again.

I CAN'T SLEEP. I was dreaming that I was forced to row a rickety rowboat all the way to Iberia. When I got there I was facing a towering stone wall set right on the beach, and it extended from the French border on the Atlantic Ocean, all the way around Spain, Portugal, and Spain again to France on the Mediterranean Sea.

It is so much better in my reading chair with a cup of coffee than it was on that cold, wet wooden bench with splintery oars. I should be hungrier, after all that activity. Maybe I didn't get as far as I thought.

I hate these dreams. I don't have to go to Iberia in daylight, and I don't want to go there when I'm asleep. I have never had any interest in the place. All it does is fill me with foreboding.

Solomon is becoming lax. I would say happy, but he doesn't seem terribly happy these days. Nor is he willing to make any decisions concerning his wedding, or it seems, the rest of his material and spiritual life. He needs a jolt.

That's why I mentioned the Inquisition to him. And he laughed. My mistake. Until I know for certain whether the Inquisition was involved in the lives of the Benevistes, I should have remained silent. But if it was, Solomon will not laugh. I will make him share my dreams of Iberia.

103

AS SOON AS I walked into the house, I could see trouble. Mother had the look. I am really tired of the look. I should develop my own look for her.

She said, "I spoke with Father Phillips. He was terribly impressed with your Solomon. He found him intelligent and charming. A bit skeptical, but he thinks that's healthy for a young man. Yes, you two put on quite a performance."

She wanted a rise, but I wouldn't do it.

She said, "Father Phillips wondered where you are planning to settle after the wedding. I told him I assume you are staying in your home town. He also wondered if you plan to join the church."

I have been a member all my life. So this was the big question. And I don't know the answer. I do not know whether Solly is going to join the church.

She said, "He is a Christian, isn't he? And as denominations go, the Episcopalians stand on top of the cake."

"You mean: move up to high test? He is Christian, Mother, but it's a lot more complicated than that."

"What's complicated? He is or he isn't."

"His family has a long difficult religious history. His mother is doing research on it right now."

"He is or he isn't."

I said, "We're getting married in the church. That's the important thing. Let's leave it at that. I don't want to make trouble."

"Since when did service to Jesus Christ become trouble?"

Standing, arms folded, eyeglasses hanging off her bosom, she had that prison warden look. I said, "What exactly do you want?"

"Father Phillips thinks your husband could have a bright future working for the church, with his mind, and his ability with numbers and finance. But of course Father Phillips wants to hire our own." Our own? "He would like Solomon to be baptised in our church."

I guess I've known this was coming since that first day, when I told her he was Jewish. But I still felt it right in the gut. I told her not to count on it. She wondered if he has sufficient faith, and I told her he isn't big on faith. Well! How can he be right for me? I said I think there are good people who don't get their strength from a church.

Mother gave me a dragon look and said, "Perhaps you would be good enough to explain this wedding you are planning. You will be in your very expensive dress, off-white, for some reason. And Father Phillips will tell you that your marriage signifies the mystery of the union between Jesus Christ and his church. The ring Solomon puts on your finger will indicate that you have bound yourselves together through Jesus Christ our Lord. Explain what this means if your husband does not believe in Jesus Christ. What is the basis of your marriage?"

"Love."

"If he truly loves you, he will accept baptism. Then you two will have a chance to become one."

"Really, Mother, do you think a splash of water will make us any closer?"

She stared a hole through my head. "A splash of water? Is that what you said?"

"I'm sorry." And I was.

"Are you questioning the value of initiation into Christ's body the Church?"

"No, Mother. I'm only questioning what it would mean to Solly right now."

I would like to give her his baptism. If I could do it when he was asleep, I would. But it doesn't count if the person is tricked into it. Or coerced—that's what I should have told her.

Mother isn't going to give this up. It's the perfect vehicle for her. By playing on my guilt she can control a wedding she isn't paying for.

A month ago I thought this wedding was going to be so easy. Now I can hardly see it working out. Who's going to be happy? Only Dad, since he's not paying attention. I started to cry.

Mother looked at me dubiously, like when I used to tell her I was too sick to go to school. I begged her: "Tell me the limos are ridiculous. My dress makes my chest look too flat. But please, don't do this to me right now."

"Do what?"

Louise Pennybaker, still the queen.

TODAY I BEGIN to follow the scent of the Benevistes toward southern Europe. Since they were like me, I know that they were forced to go, and my guess is that the boot was Portuguese. Otherwise they would have landed in a Spanish possession rather than in Brazil.

But what could they have done to merit expulsion? What kind of evil are the Benevistes capable of?

Iberian Solomon was no more a highwayman than his son was a swashbuckler in Brazil. Maybe he was a creative bookkeeper. I don't see him being deported for that. Perhaps the criminal was his wife, who watched ever-uglier official anti-Semitism threaten the family safety and livelihood, and erode her husband's enterprise, health, and will to live. Finally she found it unendurable. But what would she do?

What I keep thinking of is the Portuguese expulsion of heretics. Heresy. What would that mean to a family of merchants? We purchase, we mark up, we sell. Heresy seems a crime of another world.

TODAY WE WENT to Rubinstein's jewelers, which is owned by one of Solly's clients. All my life I've been waiting to put my nose to a case full of gold and platinum and pick something out. It would have been perfect if it felt like Solly was there with me. He was next to me, but not really.

He said, "See anything you like?"

It was like being in an ice-cream parlor. I didn't see anything I didn't like.

He said, "What color?"

"The yellow gold." I like the white gold, but that yellow means married. The plain gold band. A matching set. You hold them up against each other and nothing can go wrong.

The clerk went to get Simon Rubinstein, and Solly introduced me. "This is my fiancée, Allison."

His fiancée. I'm staring at that word on the paper. What the hell does it mean now?

Simon congratulated me. He was smooth. I pointed out what I wanted and he said, "Ah, the Evermore."

Great name. I asked if he had it in men's sizes. Then Solomon said, "You know, Allison, I don't think I'm going to get one."

Simon took my ring size and retreated to the back in a hurry. I said, "What do you mean? All this time we were going to have the same rings. You said so!"

"I did. But I tried on a ring and it was uncomfortable. I've never worn jewelry."

"In a couple of days you don't even feel it."

"I'm sorry. It's just not for me. Let's not blow this thing out of proportion. The vows don't change any." And then he tried to kiss me!

"You don't have to wear it all the time, Solly. But you should have a wedding ring." God help me, but I couldn't help thinking what my mother said: that our rings would mean nothing.

He said, "It's silly to have it if I don't wear it."

"How about if I didn't wear one either?" Like I would ever give that up.

"I won't make you. But I would like you to wear one. Does that make me evil?"

I said, "I don't know what you are any more, Solomon."

I left him in the store. I didn't get my ring. I must be the most unhappy woman in the universe.

INTERVIEW SHEET

Complaint—Follow up Information
Interviews of BFI Job Number 62—4013
Patient: Allison Pennybaker
Evaluating physician: S. Karlin

The patient is a 28—year-old unmarried white
female who presented with aphonia, inability to
speak, after witnessing a fatal fire. The fire
consumed the house of the mother of the man she
was to have married that very afternoon. The
sudden appearance of neurologic disease in the
setting of extreme psychological stress without
explanation by physical disorder or clear
pathophysiologic mechanism is most compatible
with the somatoform disorder known as conversion
disorder. Physical evaluation to date has not
suggested that neurological disease or physical
harm such as smoke inhalation could account for
the aphonia. The patient's lack of concern, or
la belle indifference, an associated feature of
conversion, is also present here.

Conversion disorder, formerly known as
hysterical neurosis, conversion type, is
classically explained using a psychological
rather than biological model. The clear temporal
relationship to the shocking stressor is
noteworthy; the physical symptom creates the
''primary gain'' of keeping a conflictual feeling

out of awareness. A symbolic linking of the symptom of the conflict is often seen. Here one could theorize that her inability to speak prevents her from acknowledging the traumatic event. So-called ''secondary gain'' may also be seen when the symptoms help the patient avoid a noxious activity and attain support. Inability to speak would then be seen as a means to avoid communication about a painful event.

There is no evidence that the symptom is intentional and with obvious goal such as in malingering. Thus it is difficult to be certain what benefit the aphasia provides her.

While conversion disorder can be of short duration with abrupt onset and resolution, recurrent conversion and underlying dependency needs may signal a more protracted course. It is therefore difficult to ascertain the prognosis.

RABBI HERTZENBERG troubles me. Maybe it's because of what he will think about me—and I know he will think about me. Maybe it's because he always insists that I come to services and roundtable discussions.

I sincerely hope he does not think it's because of HIM, Rabbi Hertzenberg, that I am returning, and not the Almighty. I deal direct.

That might be a little overboard.

Anyway, I called and told him where I lost the family tree. Could it be that the Inquisition had anything to do with our exile? He said yes, more than likely.

I said—But I can't believe that my family were criminals.

—They had to commit just one crime, and you could say it was a natural talent: acting like a Jew, or simply having Jewish blood.

—How could they not? They were Jews.

—There were no official Jews in Portugal then.

I couldn't believe it. He told me this: The original Inquisition started about 350 years before it reached Portugal. The Catholic Church was alarmed by sects who chose their own form of Christian worship, and had no need for the church hierarchy (and who does, he added). The Inquisition was established to wipe them out. Soon after that the Dominican Order made the Inquisition into a professional outfit, famous for its thoroughness, secrecy, brutality, and paperwork. This surprised me, since I always assumed that an operation like that was hushed up. He said the Inquisition was an arm of the Papacy, conducted by special Papal representatives. It was legitimate and legal. In most countries the Inquisitors wielded power which made monarchs cower. Every moment of the

Inquisitors' work was committed to paper. EVERY MOMENT.

I said—I don't know why I'm so amazed. Imagine signing your name to an Inquisitorial document.

—For hundreds of years the Inquisition was only concerned with heresy against the Church by Christians. May all of their generations drink ambrosia, if you know what I mean. Jews were not their concern. But that changed, especially in Spain and Portugal. They were the last European nations to ask for the Inquisition.

—ASK?

—The way you might invite an exterminator into your home.

—Did those countries exile people?

—Yes, many. If your family was deported from Portugal in the sixteenth century, it was the work of the Inquisition, and it most likely had to do with judaizing.

Judaizing. What a word.

He said—That meant acting in any minute way like a Jew. And I mean MINUTE.

—Even though they were all Christians.

—Right.

—But there used to be many Jews there.

—Yes. The largest Jewish population in the world at the time.

—What happened to them?

—They either converted, or left. Or died, naturally or, especially, unnaturally.

—When would the family have converted?

—In Portugal it all happened at once. 1497, a year of eternal blackness.

This meant that my family had converted, and were exiled later anyway. The thought of disentangling another forced conversion made my soul sick. What is wrong with this world?

I said—What happened to all that paperwork? Are there any records still existing?

—Almost all of them still exist. The proud Portuguese have

preserved them for five hundred years. May their wives be as fruitful as pomegranates, if you know what I mean.

—I don't know what you mean.

—I would never say anything disrespectful about the dead.

One more issue. I had thought it was wrong for me to interfere, but that just changed. I said—What do you think about joint wedding services, Jewish and Christian?

He thought for a moment—I don't love them, but I think they're better than the alternative.

—Do you conduct them?

—When necessary.

—When necessary to prevent five thousand years of Jewish civilization from being extinguished from an exceptional young man's life?

—Yes, that's when.

113

WHEN I GOT home from work there was a package at my door. I can't get too excited about wedding presents these days, since I might end up giving them all back. That will be the most humiliating moment of my life. I won't stay in this town if it happens.

It was very light for such a big box. It was filled with those little styrofoam pickle-shaped things, and they came pouring out. I dug all the way through the box and felt around and I couldn't find anything. A practical joke. Great. And now those stupid pickle things were all over my living room.

I scooped them up, but of course now they didn't all fit back in the box. As I was pushing them in, they started to make terrible shrieks. Like they were alive and I was crushing them to death. I knew nothing was really alive, but when you hear a sound like that you have to take a look.

That's when I found it. A tiny little box with a tiny little bow. I had no idea what it was. That shows how in tune I am these days.

It was the ring. The Evermore. I started to cry. If I keep going like this, I'm going to have my dress taken in, I'll be so dehydrated.

MY SON WILL BE a married man two weeks from today. Five days ago the rabbi told me there was likely a paper trail to the early days of my family. I have done nothing about it. I have never sat on a task for five days in my life, certainly nothing of this significance. I must be very afraid of what I'm going to find at the end.

Earlier today I forced myself to look into new sources. The Portuguese Inquisition: It didn't begin until 1531, even though the Spanish Inquisition had been operating since 1478. During that same year, 1531, Lisbon was largely leveled by a huge earthquake, attributed to the perfidy of the New Christians— the converted Jews. Just as I am getting one now, the New Christians got a terrible feeling about what was going to happen, and sent representatives laden with great wealth, astonishing wealth, to the Pope. This kept the Inquisition in the Pope's own control and out of the far bloodier hands of the King of Portugal.

The good fortune couldn't last. Does it ever? The Portuguese Inquisition finally won its unfettered way in 1547. Its first *auto-da-fé* had already taken place in 1540. Look at what I just wrote! So matter-of-fact. Its first *auto-da-fé*. As if it were its first board meeting, or its first company picnic. What exactly went on during these notorious events?

Over the international library computer network, I had Jenny make an inquiry to the Portuguese National Archives in Lisbon. I was certain that no answer would come; the Portuguese, or the Church, would defend the secrecy of these archives to the end.

The screen blinked and came to life, and we both jumped. We were welcomed to the Inquisition database. I still can't believe that they would let people walk right in.

The archive asked for names and dates of my inquiry. I had to guess. If there was a trial, it had to be between 1548, when the Portuguese started exiling heretics to their territories, and 1630, when the Dutch took Brazil. That was almost a hundred years.

We waited again. Quite a remarkable experience, waiting to

see if your family shows up on the heretic roll of the Portuguese Inquisition.

Finally it told us that the information is not in the principal
database. The search was going to take overnight.

What an exquisite torture! I am certain that I have come to
the right place.

THE RING DIDN'T FIT. Perfect. Solly picked me up and we went back to the store.

I said, "I don't want to get pushy. I hate women who do that. But I want everyone in the world to know that we're together. That's why I want you to wear a ring. It's a symbol of us that everybody can see."

I said this while we were still in the car so we wouldn't have another scene in public. Then I had one of those rare moments when I heard myself as if I was somebody else. I felt like telling the chick: What's the big deal? Other husbands don't have rings. It doesn't mean they don't love their wives, any more than a ring is a guarantee that they do. Bless your stars that you have such a great guy.

But then he turned to the chick and said, "OK." So we ordered an Evermore for him. I'm sure there was a reason we had to go through all that, and I'm sure I don't know what it is. And I'm sure he doesn't either.

When we got back into the car I was feeling warm and snuggly. I wanted to climb into the back seat. I had some accounts receivable I thought he might want to clear up. But something told me to keep my mouth shut.

When we got to my place he dropped me off and said he had to work tonight. We're going for the license tomorrow and he's going to miss half a day. He kissed me and he left. What is going on?

117

WHEN I OPENED the library the computer monitor was giving off an otherworldly come-to-me-you-are-in-my-power glow. And there it was, a message that there was a transmission from Portugal. My stomach began to ache. I had to turn away.

But just for a moment. This is the information I have been tracking for two months, which I will hand to my lost son in the hope that it will help him find his way. I sat in front of the computer, and there it was: a list of Benevistes who appeared before the Portuguese Inquisition starting in 1550, at all three tribunals: Evora, Coimbra, and Lisbon. My attention was drawn to one particular occasion, or rather, a group of them, lasting from 1605 to 1608. It was the Lisbon trials of an entire Beneviste family—including one couple named Juan and Maria.

These are the forebears of Maria and Juan who signed my Bible. I am sure of it.

WE HAD TO GO to town hall to get our marriage license. It's a grungy building, but I was expecting there would be a pretty little chapel in there, maybe with a little stained glass.

In my dreams. It was a dark room in the back, with pipes hanging out of the ceiling and they banged every few minutes. And it smelled bad. I thought it would smell like flowers and honeymoons. Solly pointed out that people also buy fishing licenses there.

One couple was there when we arrived. The guy looked like he was just old enough to shave. The girl looked like a cheerleader, with the great bod. I wonder if I would have married Solly if I met him that young. I'm not sure I would have recognized how incredible he is. I think God designs it so you spend a lot of time with creeps and losers when you're young. That way you appreciate the right guy when he comes along.

The girl was really excited, laughing at everything the clerk said. The guy just answered the clerk's questions. He looked nervous. Too late. The time for being nervous officially ended when he popped the question.

119

Solly was quiet too. But he can't be nervous about me. Or at least he can't doubt me, because no guy ever married a woman who loved him more than I love Solly. Maybe this is just the way men do it. They want to get married, but they do this agony thing. Then they can tell their buddies what a struggle it was. They were fighting all the way. Want to see my scars?

The clerk called us. She was about Mother's age. She wasn't smiling and she barely looked at us. It was just another form for her.

I was ready. I gave her my passport, driver's license, high school and college diplomas, and a couple of credit cards. She looked at me out the top of her glasses and said, "You're not applying for a mortgage, dear. You're just getting married."

"JUST getting married?"

The woman copied from our birth certificates onto the form. I said, "I thought you might want to see documents that show that our marriage is going to go fine."

"No."

"When you get a driver's license, they want to see that you can drive."

"Driver's license in room 203."

She asked questions: Names. Addresses. Date and location of the wedding. Would I be changing my name? Absolutely. I already have the signature.

And then questions about our parents. I answered. "Louise Rogers Pennybaker. Harold Pennybaker." I realized that a long time ago they were sitting right in this same room. She was only nineteen. She must have been out of her mind with excitement. She and Dad had never done it together. Everything was going to happen the day and night of the wedding—getting naked in front of each other, figuring out exactly who was supposed to do what. That would be too much for me. I'm glad I had my pre-wedding classes.

Solly said, "Miriam Beneviste. Aaron Beneviste. Deceased."

When the clerk was done Solly read over the form. I watched him. With his coal black hair, clear, olive complexion, strong nose he looks so different from us. Aaron and Miriam Beneviste were born in America, like Harold and Louise, but they might as well have come from different planets. I imagine some of my friends are saying that about Solly and me too. But love let us cross the borders.

Louise doesn't believe it. I'm not so sure about Miriam, either. I keep thinking that she's going discover something about the family past and it is going to march back over our borders. Is that unfair? Maybe, but when I signed the form I was wishing it was a treaty holding Miriam off for a couple of more weeks.

THE TRANSCRIPT arrived, eight hundred pages—and I'm told this one is relatively short! Here is the story:

In 1605 the Portuguese Inquisition issued an Edict of Grace. This offered people merciful treatment if they came forward to confess their crimes against Christ and the Church. A magnanimous gesture? No. My history book says that the thrust of the Edict of Grace was not the salvation of those who came forward. It was the threat behind it—to those who did not. They were being told that they could expect far sterner penalties if any unexpiated deeds were exposed by the Inquisition.

Juan Beneviste came forward during this grace period. It was the first entry in his file. His first confession is so bizarre that I've reread the translation and even scanned the original Portuguese for the few words I know. Juan Beneviste presented himself to the Inquisition to confess to: eating kosher meat. He confessed to doing it exactly three times. And changing his linens on a Saturday. This he did twice.

121

Why on earth would he confess this? The Inquisitor should have patted Juan on the head and sent him on his way. But just the opposite happened. The confession was accepted in perfect solemnity, and the Inquisitorial procedure began. I feel a chill. The radiator isn't doing any good.

At the end of his interview Juan was asked if he had anything to add. Even on paper the question is portentous. He swore that these were his only transgressions against the Church. A notary had taken down all his words, and Juan signed the transcript. It is an elegant but shaky signature.

Could he have expected that the Inquisition would let the offences pass? He learned better the next week, when he was summoned before a group of officials, including an Inquisitor. From Juan's stuttering entrance, he seemed surprised, outraged (though in a very respectful fashion). He said—I don't understand why I have been asked here. I have told you everything. This is outrageous, your Excellency! (The notary put in the exclamation point.)

The Inquisitor said—We have been enjoined by the Holy Father in Rome to save your soul from eternal damnation.

That seems to have cleared the air. The Inquisitor consulted with his prosecutors and legal counsel. Was anyone on Juan's side? I see that there was one, the advocate. That's a surprise.

Juan was asked to repeat his original confession. This was no empty exercise: any discrepancies between the two accounts would be very dangerous for him. He did well. He must have had good coaching from the advocate.

Or did he. The advocate now said this:—Juan Beneviste, confess all. Your immortal soul depends on it.

Juan:—I have told all. I've done it twice.

Advocate:—I warn you to remember the case of Beatriz Nunez.

Juan:—I don't know about any cases of the Inquisition. How would I know? I am a good Christian.

Advocate:—She confessed her heretical acts and was reconciled with the Church. Later it was discovered that she had committed heretical acts in her youth. Because she claimed not to remember them, the tribunal judged her impenitent.

This is an advocate? Back to the historical sources. I see: the task of Inquisitional advocates was not the defense of the clients, but simply to secure their confessions. They were members of the Inquisition. So much for Juan's aid.

Juan said—What happened to her?

Advocate:—She was relaxed to the secular authorities.

I imagine that every Inquisitorial examination began with a scare story. I'm surprised that this one didn't have a grimmer climax. Juan didn't bother to respond.

The Inquisitor started to speak, and I could feel the fear in the room—Juan Beneviste, you have come forward to confess your crimes against the Church. Why have you done this?

—I have made mistakes, your Excellency. I want to be reconciled to the Church.

—You are ready to confess all?

—I already have.

—You have confessed to eating food prepared in infidel

fashion, and engaging in pagan rites during the sabbath. Who else do you know, or who have you heard of, guilty of these same offences against the Lord?

—No one. Just me.

—Do you know how to murder animals in the infidel fashion? I thought you were a merchant.

—I am. I do not know the kosher laws.

—Then who prepared the infidel food you ate?

—I'm not sure. It was a feast.

—You were keeping the infidel holidays? This is a serious offence.

—No, it wasn't the holidays. I don't know when the holidays are. It was just a large meal.

—And you don't know who prepared it?

—No I don't. I arrived late.

—Who was your host?

—There was no host. Just a lot of people eating outdoors.

—Tell me about these people. Who were they?

—There were so many that I can't remember. I must have had too much wine.

Inquisitor:—Juan Beneviste! A good Christian has no secrets from the Church. Those who attempt to protect the guilty—especially those who come forward in Grace to do so—are not sincere in their penitence. Feigning allegiance to God's revealed religion is heresy, and demands a terrible punishment.

The notary, who recorded not only every word but also occasional observations about the players, now notes that sweat has soaked through Juan's doublet.

Juan:—I am no heretic. I am a good Christian. I go to church almost every Sunday. I am telling all I remember. It would be easier if I made something up to please the Inquisition, but that would be sinful. I would never do it.

Inquisitor:—I see here that your family is New Christian, with a long history of heretical activity. You are just the newest dog in the litter.

Juan:—My family is innocent! They were all baptised!

Inquisitor:—Your ancestors were brought to trial five times since the Purification of Portugal.

Juan:—But that was over one hundred years ago.

Inquisitor:—The years change nothing. The Church is timeless. Confess all and save your soul. Who do you know who participates in infidel rites? Who do you know who defames the name of the Father, the Son, and the Holy Spirit?

Juan:—No one, I swear to you.

Inquisitor:—Juan Beneviste, the Inquisition has many ears. I hope for your sake that today's session is the result of a failure of memory.

Juan:—I cannot remember what I cannot remember. No one can do that.

Inquisitor:—I am going to give you the opportunity to ponder without distraction. That way we know that memory is not the problem.

End of session. They did not tell him when he was supposed to reappear. Nor did they level threats at him. Even so, this promised to be a desperate time ahead for Juan.

Then the totally unexpected happened, I mean to me. The following two pages in Juan's file—and presumably the document that the Inquisitor was referring to when he charged Juan with being a New Christian—was the genealogy of the entire Beneviste family going back to 1497! I knew that family history was part of all Inquisitorial trials, but I didn't realize that they drew up hundreds of years worth for each prisoner. How could Juan, or anyone else, prove the purity of their spirit when there was documented proof that their blood was tainted?

Still, I have the family tree back five hundred years! They're all here, in their glorious ordinariness, all mine. Solomon will be thrilled. He had better be thrilled.

124

MOTHER CALLED before I left for work. Always a bad sign. She said, "And just what is going on with this wedding? You might have at least told me. The mother of the bride is due some respect."

"What's wrong, Mother?"

"Just a few days to break the news to our friends. Is that too much to ask? People who have known you your entire life. Has anyone bothered to ask Father Phillips? Or is he in on this little conspiracy too? Has it come to that? My own clergyman!"

"What are you talking about?"

I heard her inhale deeply. She went to an exercise class and this was all she learned. Then, slightly calmer, she said, "I called her. I didn't want to interfere. I just wanted to be sure she was receiving my invitations to dinner. I couldn't imagine why she wasn't responding."

"Mrs. Beneviste?"

"Of course."

Damn it, I told Mother to leave her to me. I said, "So did you agree to meet?"

"Yes, at the baseball game."

"That's a great idea!"

"Whether or not that is a great idea is beside the point. She had something else to tell me about your wedding service. It has been completely changed."

"That's news to me."

"I suppose you don't know about the rabbi at your wedding."

"No, Mother. Unless it's that little rabbi you like to talk about."

"She told me that this was going to be a joint service, a rabbi up on our dais side by side with Father Phillips, saying God knows what. And with all the preparation I've already done."

"I promise you, Mother. Solly and I have never even discussed it."

"I thought Solomon was going to join the church. You told me so."

"I told you I would ask him. That's all."

She said, "Is he going to be a Jew or a Christian? Does he

125

want to swear his vows to a priest or a rabbi? I think we should know already."

After my wedding class I realized that I don't care, as long as he swears them to me in front of somebody. I said, "Maybe she was just thinking out loud. She would like her child married in her faith, just like you. That's not so strange."

Then she lost it. She started screaming at me. "No, not like me! My faith is the true faith, revealed by God to earth by his son Jesus Christ. Religion is not like aspirin, every brand the same. How can you talk like this? What is he telling you? My own daughter! I have to lie down."

And she hung up. Thank God.

Of course Mother can get hysterical if a bird poops on her windshield. This was tension talking. I can't take it literally. If I did I'm not sure I'd ever speak to her again.

I called Solly, who said Miriam never said anything about a rabbi to him. Actually I think it's a nice idea. A rabbi would add color.

So why would Miriam say this to Mother? Solly thinks she was just trying to keep Mother from calling her again. I'm sure it worked. I think it's more than that. She is taking the war toward our borders, and the first shot nailed Mother good.

SOLOMON WAS angry with me, and I considered apologizing. I should never have told Louise Pennybaker about the rabbi. Not that I don't think we should have one. I do, absolutely. But I agreed to the Christian service, and it is not for me to change it without Solomon's assent.

He seems to feel that my interference is a more important matter than his willing assimilation into the Episcopalian world of crustless bread and abounding cocktails. He kept telling me what isn't my place. I accept that. But it is also not my place to pretend that my responsibility as his mother has expired because he is getting married; I'm sure he will call on it many times in years to come. It *is* my place to try to make him see something vital about his life.

And still I might have apologized to him if Louise Pennybaker hadn't happened to call me after I spent much of the night reading the transcripts of Juan Beneviste. Her tone was perfectly offensive, her smugness bottomless. She suffers my words as if I am a lost child and every thought of hers is God's will.

After a few minutes I had had enough. And so, being very careful not to say anything definitive, I mentioned to her the possibility of a rabbi at the service. Perhaps an old man with a long beard and a thick accent and a furious fur hat who would rave from her pulpit. I hoped he wouldn't say anything untoward about Jesus Christ, but it was out of my hands. And then, to be sure she knew that at heart I am really on her side, I agreed to meet at the baseball game. I left her nothing to say. It was very satisfying.

Though baseball is silly, this is an annual family event, outdoors and noisy, a good setting to discharge my responsibility. Even if Louise and I sit together, conditions will prevent the conversation from becoming too involved. The less we know each other, the more likely we will get along at the wedding. That is what I want for Solomon.

I did not suspect that the memory chamber the Inquisitor offered Juan was a solitary dungeon cell. He was left there for five weeks. Aside from the jailer, who would not speak to so loathsome a character, Juan did not see a human face for all that time.

What might Juan have been thinking? That the Inquisition could now confiscate all of his property and cast his family into the gutter. That he might well die right here, and no one outside the Inquisition would ever know. Escape? Manipulation of the jailers required lots of money, which he did not have, at least not with him. A failed escape attempt was considered a violation of the code of secrecy of the Inquisition.

And his chances for acquittal, if he ever did get a trial? It would depend on others' testimony. Most people he knew were New Christians—converted Jews. Their testimony, if it was helpful to a defendant, was inadmissible at an Inquisitorial trial. (Incriminating New Christian testimony *was* considered trustworthy.) What Old Christian would testify on behalf of a New Christian? Should the trial go against Juan, which was almost guaranteed, his supporters could be accused of concealing his sacrilege, with terrible consequences. As for the prosecution, Juan would never be told the accusations against him or the identity of those who testified. This could include people who harbored petty personal resentments, the Inquisition's many spies, or even professional perjurers, who lived off blackmail. Juan was in the absurd position of trying to refute all charges by blind conjecture of what they might be and who were leveling them. It is hardly surprising that the Portuguese Inquisition acquitted approximately two people a *year*.

Others would be testifying in other trials, and Juan's name could be mentioned. That was the danger. If someone implicated Juan in heresy before he confessed, his confession would count for little. How many of the other diners at that kosher feast were just then being grilled by an Inquisitor, or shooing away rats in a urine-soaked cell, ready to bargain?

This must have been his reason for coming forward during the Edict of Grace: he was afraid he was going to be named. There must have been an overpowering impulse to call for the jailer, to request another audience with the Inquisitor, to confess and thereby preempt someone else's account.

But there was one terrible problem. A confession would not be considered true unless he named names. That would mean imprisonment or worse for people close to him.

Juan wrestled with that problem for the entire five weeks, until he was again called to face the officials of the Inquisition. Thin, exhausted, stinking of himself, eyes blinking in the light, he faced the magnificent Inquisitor and his minions. From the transcript:

Advocate:—Confess and save your soul.

Inquisitor:—Juan Beneviste, you are again in the tribunal of the Holy Office of Rome. Has your memory been revived?

Juan:—Yes.

Inquisitor:—Tell us your confession.

Juan:—I participated in a feast where kosher food was served. I remember one other man who was there. His name was Ignatz. I don't know his last name or where he lives. He is the only one I remember.

Inquisitor:—I thought the devil was more clever than that.

Juan:—It's the truth. I am guilty. I ate the food. I am ready to do my penance.

Inquisitor:—You are not ready for anything until you have proven by your full and total confession that you have accepted Christ. Short of that, you are a heretic whose insincerity mocks the intelligence of this holy tribunal.

Juan:—Maybe it was Ignatz Ramos.

Inquisitor:—And the others?

Juan:—I didn't know them.

Inquisitor:—You seem to be having problems with your memory again.

Juan:—No!

Inquisitor:—Juan Beneviste, we are in the business of saving souls. The body, to us, is just a conveyance of the soul and means little. If the body has to suffer to save the soul, so be it.

Juan:—What are you going to do to me?

Advocate:—Save your soul!

Juan:—For God's sake, I've just been in hell. Have mercy!
Inquisitor:—Confess.
Juan:—I have. God knows, I have.
Inquisitor:—My God knows you have not.

MOTHER CALLED late this evening. She was perfectly calm, she said. She just wanted to know about the rabbi at the wedding. I told her there isn't going to be one. She said it's better for her to know now than to be surprised. She's not good at surprises. She refuses to believe me. She is locked up in some paranoid fantasy.

Solly made a face when he heard it was her. He's already sick of the subject.

She said, "I know you would protect your husband, as a wife should. But what a situation for me! After all these years of service to the church. What will I say to them?"

That did it. I pushed the phone into Solly's hand, and he was stuck. She told him how bad it would be to have a family divided in religions, how confusing for the children. Look at the influence of Christianity all over the world. If not for the New Testament we would all be running around in loin cloths, fornicating with wild beasts. He smiled at that. He said that the wedding service would be Christian, and then we'll see. He wouldn't let her pin him down. She told him that Father Phillips wanted him to join the church. He could have a future in the leadership. He said he was flattered, but he didn't care much for the idea of joining, or converting. But we could talk about it after the wedding. He was wonderful.

As far as I'm concerned, the religious stuff is settled.

POLICE LABORATORY ANALYSIS
REPORT

BFI Job Number 62—4013
Received from fire marshal: M. Hazel
Chemist/technician: S. Benjamin

1. Burned flooring from basement shows significant traces of unleaded gasoline.

2. Burned ceiling tile shows infiltration of smoke from gasoline fire. No infiltration of gasoline. Identical results found on stairway riser and runner.

3. Both cans contain traces of gasoline identical to that found on floor.

4. Handcuffs are common commercial model, not designed for law enforcement. Shows fingerprints of Miriam Beneviste and Solomon Beneviste. Burned flesh found around perimeter of one of cuffs.

THE NEXT ENTRY describes Juan after three more months in solitary confinement, in heavy chains. He must have been close to insane. Now he was facing more serious accusations.

Inquisitor:—Juan Beneviste, you are charged with practicing infidel Sabbath rites, with participating in feasts celebrating the torture of our Lord Jesus Christ, in relieving yourself on a holy crucifix, in denying the virginity of the Holy Mother . . .

Juan began to defend himself vigorously against the new, false charges. But they were so numerous, and he was so exhausted, that he did not address them all. In the eyes of the Inquisition, he was guilty of every offence he did not disavow. This was standard procedure.

There was enough legal formality to the tribunal that the Inquisitor could not convict Juan. But he would, there was no doubt of that. Which is why I am wearing a warm scarf while I sit in my living room.

Juan did not return to the dungeon alone. The law mandated that the entire Inquisitorial entourage accompany him.

Juan:—Where are we? For the love of God, why have you brought me here?

Inquisitor:—To save your soul. Remove his clothes.

Juan:—By whose authority? This is outrageous. Take your hands off me!

Inquisitor:—Juan Beneviste, I adjure you to tell the truth. We were not sent here by the Holy See to make you suffer. Spare us this and tell us all you know. Cleanse yourself. Find yourself in Christ's truth.

Juan:—Not so tight. God, you're cutting off my circulation.

The executioner was binding Juan's hands behind his back. Juan knew what was coming, the torture known as *strappado*.

Despite the secrecy to which all victims of the Inquisition were sworn, its techniques were common knowledge.

Then a terrible scream. By means of a pulley at the ceiling, a rope attached to Juan's bound wrists was pulled by the executioner, and Juan was jerked into the air.

Inquisitor:—Confess.

Juan:—Ahhh! You're killing me! Let me down!

The Inquisitor signaled the executioner to lift him higher. The room echoed with Juan's screams. The pain was so great that he soiled himself. This the notary made sure to record.

Inquisitor:—Confess. Save yourself. Spare us this unpleasantness.

Juan:—All right. All right.

He was lowered so just his toes touched the floor.

Inquisitor:—Go ahead.

Juan:—It was Ignatz Ramos. He cooked the meal.

Inquisitor:—What else?

Juan:—That's all. Now you must believe me.

At the Inquisitor's direction, the executioner tied two heavy weights to Juan's ankles, and again he was jerked into the air.

Juan swore and begged. In a minute he succumbed. He told them the names of twenty-two people at the dinner. He admitted to a lifetime of secret Jewish observance. He told them that his wife had taught Hebrew language and practices to their children. This seems to have been what the Inquisitor expected to hear.

The following day Juan was again brought to face the Inquisitor.

Inquisitor:—Listen carefully.

The notary read Juan's confession back to him. What must that have felt like, to have a smug, well-fed, well-oiled minion hurl your own weakness back in your face?

Inquisitor:—Do you, Juan Beneviste, swear under oath that this confession is correct in every detail.

Juan:—(Indistinct)

Inquisitor:—Repeat that so everyone can hear. With this

confession you have purged your soul and found yourself in Christ. Be grateful.

Juan:—Be grateful. All right, I am grateful. I gratefully swear that this confession is correct.

Inquisitor:—In every detail?

Juan:—In every detail.

The notary records that he was crying.

Inquisitor:—Juan Beneviste, do you swear under oath that this confession was given freely, not through coercion or fear of torture, but from your love of truth? Hold your head up when you speak.

Juan:—Yes, yes. A hundred times! Yes. It was my love of truth. God help me, what have I done?

According to the Church, a confession obtained by use or threat of torture was invalid. Thus the torture was so horrible that victims would swear anything, even this, to avoid suffering it again. God have mercy on Juan! And on the twenty-two people whose names were now in the hands of the Inquisition—especially on Maria, his wife. I fear most for her.

135

Finally the Inquisitor told Juan to get on his knees. He was so stiff from three months in a cold, dank cell that his knees would not bend. The Inquisitor pushed, and he fell to the floor.

Inquisitor:—Get up!

Juan:—Help me. Please.

Inquisitor:—Rise, infidel! You are insulting this tribunal.

Juan pulled himself up by a leg of the table. The Inquisitor held up a silver crucifix—Juan Beneviste, swear on the cross of Jesus Christ that you accept the Catholic religion in every detail.

Juan:—I accept the Catholic religion.

Inquisitor:—Juan Beneviste, swear that you anathematize all heresy against the Catholic Church.

Juan:—Yes. Please let me rise. My knees!

Inquisitor:—Stay! Juan Beneviste, do you accept the punishment the tribunal shall impose on you as just token of your penitence?

Juan:—Yes. Yes. I accept it.
But not I.

SOLLY HAD DINNER with Miriam. She told him that their family was Christian in the sixteenth century. Thank God! This should settle it for Mother. He said that their ancestors converted in the fifteenth century. Everyone in Portugal did. The Portuguese and the Spanish had a special name for the forced converts. They were called *marranos*. Which I thought sounded rather nice, until he told me what it means: Swine. Pigs.

He said, "You know, people have been calling Jews vile things for thousands of years. There's nothing new in that. But once they've converted, you'd think people would cut them a break."

"Does that make you feel bad?"

"No, but I'm sure it made them feel bad."

I had a spasm of guilt about this. Maybe guilt is the wrong word. Concern, about all this religious suffering. Without really thinking I said, "Maybe we should go to town hall for a civil ceremony."

He said, "Your mother would die of shame."

"But it would be easier on your mother."

"Don't worry about her. She's a survivor."

"But how about you, Solly? Would you like that better? We can still do it. I guess I never gave you a chance to tell me what you want."

137

I know he would prefer town hall, but he didn't say so. He agreed to the church, and I love him for it. Why is it so important to me? I guess my whole life is there. I remember watching weddings twenty years ago wondering what it would be like when it was my turn. It isn't really a religious thing. Maybe part of it is, but more of it is sentimental. Weddings are sentimental.

I want to be sure that Solly doesn't pay a price for doing this my way. I don't want him to feel like I'm turning him into a swine while he walks down the aisle of the Church of the Ascension.

MARIA BENEVISTE, wife and second cousin of Juan (the later couple in wild Brazil were first cousins), was arrested five months after he had been. He was still in prison. She did not know the charges against her.

Inquisitor:—Maria Beneviste, you have been brought before this tribunal of the Holy See to confess to your crimes and save your soul.

I thought she would be unnerved. She must have suspected that the Inquisition was holding her husband all this time. She stood silently before him.

Inquisitor:—You are mute?

Maria:—I am not mute. I have nothing to confess.

Inquisitor:—We know all about you. The only way to save yourself is to confess.

Maria:—I don't wish to take up the tribunal's time. I have nothing to confess.

She was locked in a solitary cell for two months, without being told why. This was the method of the Inquisition: the isolated prisoner was supposed to conduct a demoralizing search through her soul for every possible source of guilt (real or concocted). This method also encouraged accusations, since those who leveled them were never confronted in court.

Where would she start? The Inquisition considered guilty those who (from hundreds of examples): lit lamps or wore clean clothes on Saturday, cleaned their houses or cooked on Friday, placed their hands on the heads of their juniors without making the sign of the cross, cut their nails and kept or buried the parings, didn't eat rabbit or eel, or turned toward the wall as they die. Unbelievable? Every *marrano* knew about the man who cleaned off his father's soiled corpse and changed his shirt before burial; accused of preparing the corpse in Jewish fashion, the son died in a prison of the Inquisition. There were thousands of stories like it.

Maria was summoned back before the Inquisitor, and the interview went much the same as the first. She was returned to her cell, this time in chains, and left there for another five months. It is so easy to write: five months. If they locked her up when the daisies were first opening, the land would be deep in snow by the time she emerged. Imagine five months alone in a dank, vermin-infested room, in cold, heavy iron chains. I don't know how people lived through it. She also had to know that judaizing was considered a hereditary crime, and conviction would exclude her descendants from the church, medicine, education, and law, among other livelihoods. They would be forbidden from wearing jewelry, or riding on horseback. They were marked forever. And they were still just children. Animals!

For a third time Maria faced the Inquisitor. She must have been hunched, ill, thin, blinking, weeping from innumerable bites and sores. I can't help thinking that she was not only covered by excrement, but also blood from her menses. That these horrid men should see her this way!

Inquisitor:—Are you ready to confess your crimes against Jesus Christ?

Maria:—I have committed no crimes.

Inquisitor:—Every day there is more testimony against you. Why are you so foolish? You could be helping yourself by telling what you know. Your silence is impertinent. We must assume the worst.

Maria:—In doing so you would be making a mistake.

Inquisitor:—If we must, we will free your soul from your impertinent body. Were that not necessary.

Maria:—It is only necessary if you make it so. I have done nothing wrong.

Inquisitor:—You are a very resolute woman.

Maria:—I am God-fearing.

Inquisitor:—We'll see what you fear.

The entourage accompanied her to the dungeon. The executioner bound her hands behind her, then lifted her by a rope to the ceiling and left her there. The torture lasted an hour, ending only when she passed out.

When she came to, the Inquisitor continued:—I ask you for your own good. Confess.

Maria:—It is only for your good if I confess.

She was carried to the corner of the dungeon where there was a fire burning. The shreds of her shoes were removed and a sulfuric compound painted on the soles of her feet. While his helper held her down, the executioner extended her feet, one at a time, into the fire. The compound caught fire, the burning sensation, I've read, is likened to the fires of hell.

Maria screamed—My God, my God! You're killing me!

Advocate:—Repent!

Maria:—You are mad! Let me go! My feet are on fire! Water!

Inquisitor:—Will you repent?

Maria:—I have nothing to repent. Stop!

The notary records the stench of burning flesh. The Inquisitor made the executioner hold her to the fire until the doctor intervened. There was usually a doctor present to prevent deaths by torture. The Inquisition preferred that prisoners decompose in their cells.

Maria was told to return to her cell, but of course she could not walk.

Inquisitor:—If you stay in this chamber we must assume that you wish to continue your purification.

She crawled across the stone floor, down the stairs, and back into her little cell. The notary says it took a long time. Two weeks later, when Maria was deemed alert enough to suffer again, the executioner carried her back to the chamber and tied her onto an *escalera*, a horizontal trestle with razor-sharp rungs. Her arms and legs were secured to the sides with sharp cords which were twisted like tourniquets.

Inquisitor:—Maria Beneviste, spare yourself any more pain. Confess.

Maria:—I must be terribly important to you to go through all this bother.

Inquisitor:—All souls are important to the Church.

Maria:—Even if you have to kill them.

Inquisitor:—The soul is immortal. I am trying to set it free.

Maria:—I have nothing to confess.

Inquisitor:—Your husband has told us the truth, and by so

confessing he will be reconciled to the Church. Only the penitent ever leave here. Confess and you can leave with him.

What could she be thinking now, as the executioner was fastening her head to the *escalera*? Was it true? Did Juan give her up to the Inquisition? Would he be returning to their family? What a wonderful thought! But at her expense? What if she confessed? She could go too. Or could she? Maybe the Inquisitor was lying about Juan. Once she spoke it would be too late—she and everyone she spoke of would be condemned.

An iron prong was forced into her mouth, pushing it open almost to the breaking point. Then the executioner stuffed a strip of linen down her throat. He slowly poured water onto the strip, which blocked her trachea. She had no choice but to inhale the water, making her feel that she was strangling, suffocating. She fought to swallow. The executioner kept up a constant flow, giving her no relief. She gasped and screamed. The notary records that she passed in and out of consciousness. Foam from the struggle filled her mouth. Though she tried to talk several times, the Inquisitor commanded the executioner to continue until the first jar was empty. One jar, about one quart, was a common dose for a woman prisoner.

141

Then the Inquisitor ordered the linen strip removed from her throat. He said:—Are you ready to confess?

Maria:—Infamous man! Does your merciful Jesus Christ approve of this?

Inquisitor:—Isn't he yours as well?

The notary records that Maria was weeping furiously as she struggled for breath.

Inquisitor:—Who else will save you if not the son of God?

Maria:—Save me? What does that mean? I live according to the commandments handed down to Moses. Do you think you can improve on God's law with silly words about confession and salvation? Impious little men!

Inquisitor:—Then you confess you are a Jew! A pure heretic!

Maria:—You torturers and murderers are the heretics.

Now that he had her confession—though not the one he was after, dripping with remorse—the Inquisitor could return her to her cell. No. He ordered the linen replaced and five more quarts of water were poured down her throat. The executioner was commanded to lean all his weight on her stomach to maximize her agony. At the end of the session she crawled back to her cell, soaked in vomit.

I have an image of myself carrying Maria's tortured body beneath the portcullis and out of the castle. I am her savior. I can't help but wonder how I would have held up in Maria's place, as the executioner stripped off my shirt and hoisted me to the ceiling? I want desperately to think that I would have been just as resolute in my belief.

But what is my belief? Why don't I know? Maybe because my life has been too easy, and men in robes have never forced me back on my faith. But I should not need a torture chamber to know what I believe.

I do know that if my Solomon were brought before the Inquisition, he would break like an egg. I love him more than my own life, but I know he could not bear what Maria did, or maybe even what Juan did. And that's fine. He doesn't have to be a hero. Just a good man, and he is a good man. But he and I have missed something terribly important.

TODAY MARKED Louise Pennybaker's greatest triumph, and I am sick. Ever since Mrs. Beneviste scared her she keeps talking about Solly getting baptised. (This would keep rabbis away from the church.) I reminded her that he won't think about joining the church until after the wedding. She can ask him then.

She said it wasn't her place to ask him. Another first—something that isn't Mother's place. That means she wants me to do it. I said I won't. I don't care if he's baptised. She was outraged. Too bad. That's the end of it.

But it wasn't. I made dinner for Solly this evening. A steak, baked potato, salad, even rice pudding, homemade. All his favorites. I want to get things back on keel. After dinner we started watching some stupid game on TV, but he turned it off at halftime. He had the look again, like the Solly who had me walking funny for a month after I met him.

I took the phone off the hook. Otherwise Mother's groin antenna would have gone off and she would have called.

It was the hottest time of my entire life. (That's right, Mother. Enjoy every word.) Maybe because it was so long since the last time. Maybe because we finally put the religion stuff behind us. Whatever it was, this time I ended up feeling like I didn't know who I was. Solly and I became one body, one person. It was unbelievable.

Afterwards I was on top of him. That's probably the only thing in the world I was sure of. A sweat stain was spreading on the sheet next to him. I, who usually do no more than glow, was sweating too. It beaded on my breasts and ran down and made drops on my nipples. What a feeling! I watched the drops fall onto Solly and it was magical, the way they hit his skin. I leaned over him so my sweat dripped on his face.

He said, "What's that you're saying?"

This was weird, because I didn't realize I was talking. I thought about what was running through my mind and I said it out loud. "The courage to will and to persevere, a spirit to know and to love you, and the gift of joy and wonder in all your works."

"That's beautiful."

"Amen."

"Amen?"

"That's how it ends." And God help me, I wasn't thinking about what I was saying. I was in a trance. I was just repeating it.

"What is it, a poem?"

I had to stop and run it backwards. Then I remembered. "It's from the Book of Common Prayer. Isn't it beautiful?"

"It sounds like a prayer. What's it about?"

I didn't know the whole passage. "Heavenly Father, give them an inquiring and discerning heart, the courage to will and to persevere, a spirit to know and to love you, and the gift of joy and wonder in all your works. Amen."

"And then what?"

I moved my finger across his forehead making an X. I didn't even think about what I was doing. I mean, we were still making love.

I actually let this pass my lips: "Solomon Beneviste, you are sealed by the Holy Spirit in Baptism and marked as Christ's own for ever. Amen."

144

Suddenly I was on the bed and he was standing on the floor next to me. My inside hurt, he came out so fast. He said, "You're baptising me?" I reached for him, but he moved away. "You're baptising me while we make love?"

"No, of course not. Come back here."

"What you were repeating while we made love was a prayer of baptism, wasn't it? Were you making a cross on my forehead?"

"No. I swear. I was just wiping my sweat. Please come back."

"You have betrayed me."

That went right through my heart. I said, "I love you. YOU. I don't care what religion you are."

"But you must. This proves it."

"Come back to bed."

"You like the idea of me as a swine."

"Then I'll be a swine with you."

I reached for his arm, but he pulled it from my hand. He was putting his clothes back on. That incredible feeling I had in the center of my body a minute ago was now a spear of ice.

I couldn't let him go out the door like this. It would be the end of everything. I jumped out of bed and pulled the shirt out of his hand. I said, "I'm sorry. Please forgive me. Mother has my head all turned around these days. You know I didn't mean it. Just come back to bed."

"You've violated me in a way I didn't know was possible." He took the shirt back and started to put it on. I have never felt such terror. My whole world was ending.

I leaped at his neck and raked my nails across that scab I had made with Trudy's charm bracelet. Blood quickly started to run.

I stood in front of him. I knew what was going to happen. He screamed and put a hand to his neck and saw the blood. He smacked me across the face. Once, twice, three times. My neck twisted each time. I didn't cry.

He stopped and stared at me. Then he shuddered and fell to his knees. He moaned, "I can't believe it. I've done it again. I'm not fit to live."

I left him alone for a second. Then I knelt over him. My face was burning, but I knew he couldn't leave now.

I said, "I'm sorry, Solly. Please forgive me." I started kissing the blood on his neck.

He was crying. "How can you ever forgive me?"

"I love you so much."

"God! Me too."

We were hugging and he was making me warm. Somehow we got back into the bed, and then he carried me even further off into the universe. I can't believe this happened, since it is so sick. But I've never been so turned on in my life. So, Mother, you won about the baptism. I just hope you like the way I did it.

145

OFFICE OF MEDICAL EXAMINER

REPORT OF AUTOPSY
BFI Job Number 62—4013
Received from fire marshal: M. Hazel

I hereby certify that I, Malcolm Arthur, MD, have
performed an autopsy on the bodies of an unknown
white male and an unknown white female at the
county mortuary. The findings on the two are
identical.

External examination

The male body weighed approximately 165 pounds
and measures approximately 5' 10". The female
body weighed approximately 120 pounds and
measures approximately 5' 4". Both bodies charred
with unrecognizable features, with completely
burned soft tissue of the head, face, and neck,
and very deep thermal injury of the abdomen and
lower extremities up to the level of the bones.
Bones also charred, in many places fractured due
to thermal injury. Deep burn at the chest, some
ribs charred and fractured, deep thermal injury
of the abdomen and lower extremities. Irregular
pattern of deepest burning has character of
accelerant spilled directly on bodies.

Internal examination

Both brains have yellowish pink discoloration due
to thermal injuries. Large respiratory bronchi
have soot. Medium and small bronchi are filled with
mucoid contents. Other organs reveal no damage
or abnormality except thermal.

Cause of death

Smoke inhalation and thermal injuries of 100% of
body surface.

Manner of death

Unknown

Remarks: Of the third cadaver only a cranium was
presented (to be examined separately). Its
skeletal frame was not, as was thought,
intermixed with the remains of these two
cadavers.

147

I'M CERTAIN THAT Juan and Maria thought about each other a great deal as they sat chained in their cells. They could not think about their sentences, because convicts were not told their sentences. I take that back. The Inquisition had no convicts; it had penitents. It did not mete out punishment; it meted out penance, strictly for the good of the sinner. The penitents were destined to learn their fates in public, in spectacular fashion. This was the *auto-da-fé*.

After a wait of two more years (two years! where were the children?) after Maria's torture, penance day finally came for her and Juan. I'm so cold I can't bear it. Early in the morning of the Holy Day of Saint Mary the Virgin a bellman and town crier wove their way through Lisbon declaring that the *auto-da-fé* was at hand. In fact the Inquisition advertised spiritual benefits to those who attended (and scheduled most *auto-da-fés* on holidays). People flocked in from distant areas by the tens of thousands, sometimes up to 150,000, an astonishing number in so small a country. The *auto-da-fé* rivaled the bull-fight as the greatest popular entertainment of the time.

To drummers and trumpeters, the procession began. What a treat for those who lined the route four or five deep! First came the soldiers in armor, the August sun gleaming off their polished breastplates. Some rode mighty steeds. Then came the clergy, nearly every priest in Lisbon, almost a thousand. People cheered them though many, I'm sure, feared them. They carried a large cross shrouded in black, the standard of the Inquisition.

Behind the priests followed the penitents themselves, over seven hundred of them. They walked one by one, each flanked by two familiars, officials of the Inquisition. They probably stretched out for over a mile. I wonder if the Inquisition ever measured its achievements by the mile.

Juan and Maria were nowhere near the beginning of the line, because it was arranged in order of increasing godlessness. The impostors came first, followed by impersonators of officials of the Inquisition, blasphemers, and then the bigamists. (Those two groups should be reversed.)

Then came Juan, in a group of 264 judaizers. What could this have been like? There was no possibility of escape from his two silent companions, whose eyes never left him. That was just as well, because the crowd was howling for his (and everyone else's) blood. He and all of the penitents were dressed in a *sanbenito*, a long yellow gown marked with a large black cross, and a matching yellow miter, the tall hat like the pope's. Juan might be condemned to wear this humiliating outfit indefinitely; whatever his sentence, the *sanbenito* with his name prominently inscribed would hang in his parish church to reflect his odium on his descendants—my ancestors— hundreds of years after his death. Painted on Juan's *sanbenito* was a fire with its flames pointing downward. This meant that his confession had spared him from the fate of the flames. I doubt that anything ever quelled the fire of shame and rage burning in his heart.

Next an even more bizarre sight: the effigies, nearly two hundred of them. These were life-size dolls, in *sanbenito*, of people who were condemned by the Inquisition but had eluded it. While some had fled, most had died, especially in prison or during torture. Next in the procession came wooden chests containing the bones of these deceased, some fresh from the grave. The dead were condemned so that the Inquisition could seize all property belonging to their descendants.

Last and most godless were Maria and her group of twenty-two. Painted on her *sanbenito* was a group of devils thrusting heretics into the fires of hell. That meant that she was doomed. I can't bear this. I must have been hoping that she would find some way to survive. Did I want her to confess to false penitence? No, but I don't want her to die this way. The familiars

149

who flanked her spent the entire procession trying to exact an eleventh hour confession. I don't know if I want them to succeed.

Last in the pageant were the Inquisitors themselves, resplendent in their velvet robes. The pageant filed into the central square filled with spectacular constructions, paid for, like all Inquisitorial activity, by the property of penitents themselves, long before they ever came to trial. (And small wonder that no one was acquitted.) Many thousands of spectators packed in around them.

The honor of the first speech fell to the Archbishop of Lisbon. He commented proudly that this was the largest *auto-da-fé* since the one in Toledo in 1560, which celebrated the marriage of Philip II of Spain and Isabella of Valois. Visiting dignitaries were offered the high religious honor of lighting the brand that set ablaze the great pyre.

Then the sentencing of the seven hundred began. Even now, Juan and the others, except for Maria and the impenitent heretics, had no idea of their fates. One at a time they were brought out to hear their sentences publicly read, with thoroughness characteristic of the Inquisition. As a result, an entire day and night of sentencing passed before Juan was called.

What must he have been thinking, standing all day in the brutal Portuguese summer, and then through the chilly night, watching shabby, hungry, absurdly costumed men and women guilty of nothing except their faith sent off to grisly destinies by the plump, arrogant, velvet-draped official? All that Juan knew for certain was that he was not going to burn. Burning wasn't necessarily the cruelest fate. At least it was brief. He could spend the rest of his life in a dungeon. That was common. He could be sentenced to the galleys of the Portuguese navy, which he knew he would not survive for long. But there were lesser penalties too. Perhaps he would be rewarded for the paltry resistance he put up during his interrogation.

At seven the next morning Juan was called. He stood up, his familiars still at his side. Something like 50,000 spectators were wishing him the most brutal punishment. But worse, even if he hadn't seen her he must have sensed that Maria was there too.

From the transcript:—The Inquisitors in ordinary and Deputies of the Holy Inquisition are agreed to take into consideration of errors and confessions of Juan Beneviste, husband of Maria. (Here the entire defamed Beneviste lineage was listed.) Being a baptized Christian, and as such obliged to hold and believe all that the Holy Mother Church of Rome holds, believes, and teaches, he adopted the Law of Moses and professed it, and not the Faith of Christ, Our Lord, in whom he did not believe, nor hold Him to be the true God, the Messiah promised in the Law, but still waited for Him, as do the Jews: and believed only in the God of Abraham, Isaac, and Jacob, Creator of heaven and earth, who gave the Law to the people of Israel, and to Him he commended himself by Jewish prayers; and in observance of the said Law he kept the Sabbath on Friday afternoon, doing no work on that day, wearing his best clothes and clean linen; secretly celebrating the Jewish holy days, in particular Passover in memory of the exodus of the people of Israel from Egypt, eating unleavened bread . . . (Then followed a list of all the major holidays he confessed to observing and their unholy significances.) Behaving only exteriorly as a Catholic, in dissimulation and conformity whilst among them, attending churches and performing acts and outward observances of a Catholic Christian, knowing that the aforesaid Law of Moses was contrary to that which the Holy Mother Church of Rome holds . . . (And so on. All of this being considered, they declared:) The offender Juan Beneviste was a heretic and apostate from our holy Catholic faith, and that he has incurred the sentence of major excommunication and confiscation of all his goods to the Royal Treasury. But seeing that following better counsel he confessed his faults to the tribunal of the Holy Office with signs of repentance, asking pardon and mercy, they receive the offender Juan Beneviste into the fold, and into union with holy Mother Church, as he asks. And in penalty, and in penance for his faults they command that he shall appear in the *auto-da-fé* in customary manner, and shall formally abjure his heretical errors. And they assign him to be scourged in the number of two hundred lashes, and then to be exiled from the kingdom of Portugal proper. And he shall perform all other spiritual pains and penalties that may be imposed on him.

Juan kneeled and said this (and how long must he have practiced?):—I, Juan Beneviste, in presence of your Worships, take oath upon the Holy Gospels, on which I place my hand, that of my own free will, I do anathematize, and reject every kind of heresy that has been or may be put forward against our holy Catholic Faith and the Apostolic See, especially those into which I fell and which have been here read to me in my sentence, which I hold to be here repeated and set forth, and I swear ever to hold and to keep the holy Catholic Faith, as it is held and taught by the holy Mother Church of Rome, and that I will be ever most obedient to our most holy Father in Rome . . .

152

Did he feel he had betrayed his faith, or did he really dispense with it? Or was he content because he had stayed alive? Did he think that Maria understood why he had named her?

I think I know how Maria felt. Listening to him she died for the first time that day. This is as much of her suffering as I can bear right now.

I BOUGHT LUNCH for Jeffrey today, and I got way more than I bargained for. I wanted to check that everything on his end was under control. He was offended—have I ever failed you before? I said: Did I ever get married before? And I had a few little things to ask. Like could the ushers please wait until after the ceremony to start drinking.

He said, "You didn't say anything about that. Who's going to come to your wedding sober?"

What was the use? He's going to do what he wants. I started telling him about the limousines and the flowers and the photographer and the caterer. He spends so much time partying that he knows a lot about it. If I was messing up he would tell me.

Jeffrey said, "No one told you to get married."

"Maybe you really don't listen to Mother any more."

"Think how much wealthier you'd be. You could have a new car. A nice one. A Beamer."

"How do you get that?"

"Duh! Spend the money on the car instead of the ceremony."

"What money?"

"You must be having too much congress these days: the money for the wedding."

"And where would I get this money?"

"From your parents." He smacked his forehead like I was a complete idiot.

I said, "Why would they give me money for a car? They're hardly giving me anything for the wedding."

He started, nearly spitting out his martini. "They what?"

"What did you think?"

"I thought they were footing the bill. It's the custom."

"Mother said they'll give me what they can, but it isn't much."

"I can't believe this. You mean Solomon is paying for your wedding?"

"With help from his mother."

"Outrageous!"

"Why is it outrageous?"

And then Jeffrey said, "Because they can afford it."

"How do you know?"

153

Daniel Evan Weiss

"My buddy Ron set up their retirement account. They've been socking it away for thirty-five years, and they have quite a stash."

This left me speechless. Mouth open, hands open. I just couldn't believe it.

He said, "Don't you think they ever expected you to get married? I hate to have to say this, but you're not really that horrible."

I said, "Let me get this right. They have the money."

"Yes."

"Then why wouldn't they give it to me? Don't they care if I have a decent wedding?"

"Very much. Mother would be humiliated if you didn't."

"But weddings cost money."

"That's right."

"Where was I supposed to come up with the money?"

He looked at me. "What do you think?"

"They planned on Mrs. Beneviste, a widow, paying? You can't believe that."

Jeffrey said, "Wake up. The important part isn't that she's a widow. It's that she's one of THEM."

I sent Jeffrey away. I swore into the air in the restaurant, and everybody looked at me. What really bothered me was that I half suspected this all along, but I couldn't bring myself to believe it of Mother. Or Dad. She had to convince him, because this definitely isn't his style. What a stooge I am.

That does it. Mother and I are on opposite sides now. I would make her eat this one, but I can't without information from Jeffrey. No matter what he says, he's still afraid of her. So be it. I'll find a way to make this right on my own.

OFFICE OF MEDICAL EXAMINER

POSTMORTEM DENTAL EXAMINATION
BFI Job Number 62—4013
Antemortem dental records obtained from Dr A.
Klein.

1. Unknown male
Antemortem radiographs show amalgam fillings in
#2, #3, #14, #15, #18, #19, #20, #30, #31. #1,
#16, #17, but not #30 extracted. Their structure
compares exactly with radiographs of the
deceased.

155

2. Unknown female
Antemortem radiographs show amalgam fillings in
#2, #3, #14, #15. Gold crowns on #30, #31, #18,
#19. All molars extracted. Partial denture on #27
shows discoloration and cracking. All
structures compare exactly with radiographs of
the deceased.

This is to certify that I, S. Berkowitz DDS, have
compared the records of Dr A. Klein, including
radiographs taken within last year, to the
dentition and post-mortem examination of male
and female/unknown, BFI job no. 62—4013. I am of
the opinion that the dentitions bear sufficient
points of similarity to identify the deceased as
(1) Solomon Beneviste and (2) Miriam Beneviste.

THE NEXT DAY Juan was stripped to the waist, and placed, hands tied, astride an ass. He wore a miter bearing his name and spelling out his offence. An iron fork was fitted to his chin, preventing him from denying the crowd the pleasure of his tears and screams.

And plenty of tears and screams there probably were. While his ass was led through the streets of Lisbon, an executioner ripped into his back two hundred times with a leather strap. The onlookers gleefully counted out every blow so that Juan received his full penance.

He was returned to the prison cell. Within two months he left for Brazil and became the first of our Benevistes in the New World. There he would raise a family who would remain for some forty years, until they were driven to Curaçao; there the family would remain for forty more years, as *marranos*, until they could exhale in freedom in Newport.

By the end of the second day of the *auto-da-fé* the orator was pronouncing execrations to each of the effigies and the boxes of bones. I wish the wild absurdity could have released Maria from fear. But I know it didn't.

Finally came the last group, the pertinacious impenitent heretics. The crowd, which had thinned during the afternoon of the second day, again stuffed the square.

I'm not going to copy down the charges against Maria, since they were virtually the same as the ones against Juan. The difference was that she did not follow better counsel, did not confess faults, did not reject every kind of heresy against the Church, did not ask to be returned to its fold, and did not promise to be obedient to the most holy Father in Rome.

The Inquisitorial official read from the Book of John:—If a man abide not in me, he is cast forth as a branch and is withered: and men gather them and cast them into the fire, and they are burned—I wonder what Jesus would think of this interpretation.

Maria must have been aghast that her life could be sacrificed to this loathsome papal joke. She would never see her children again, never sit in her house and laugh with Juan, or make love with him again. It must have been virtually impossible for her to believe.

With her were twelve women and nine men. According to my histories, women were more likely to die for their faith than were men. It doesn't surprise me. Women feel more deeply than men, and they are morally stronger. One of the women was in her eighties, one was in her teens, and mercy for them was never considered. One man swore that he had done nothing, that he was a good Catholic and had always been. He may well have been telling the truth—if he refused to confess to some charge, regardless of its truth, he would still be considered a pertinacious impenitent. There was no innocence at an *auto-da-fé*.

The Roman Catholic Church, sower of love, did not execute people. Maria and the others were now officially "relaxed" into the arms of the secular authorities. Relaxed! So that's what that word means! Why should the Inquisition duck behind this euphemism after cock-strutting about during the *auto-da-fé*? More strange Inquisitorial idiom: Of the magistrate who was going to kill Maria, the Inquisition "asked and charged him most affectionately to treat her benignantly and mercifully." Did anyone sleep more easily for this?

A detachment of soldiers conveyed the twenty-two charges to the *quemadero*, the place of burning, outside of the city walls. If not for the soldiers, the inflamed crowd would have put them to a violent death. The heretics might have preferred to die this way, quickly. But the Inquisition would not be denied its spectacle. The crowd flowed from the city square

157

to the *quemadero*. Windows in houses with a good view of the *quemadero* were rented at high prices.

A priest made a final appeal to Maria to confess and save her soul. She repeated that because she had lived her life according to God's commandments, her soul was in no danger; and if it was, there was nothing that he could do about it. The priest cursed her. She was tied to a wooden post, with a huge pile of twigs, branches, and logs piled up around her.

Another woman at the *quemadero* broke in front of the immense bonfire. She took the priest's advice to confess to heresy. I can hardly blame her.

But what benefit did this yield her? No Christian could be burned alive, and the confession proved her Christian. But no one was taken away from the *quemadero*. All her Christianity meant for her, at this point, was that an iron collar, a *garrotte*, was placed around her neck and tightened until she suffocated or her spinal cord was crushed. Unless the executioner received a proper bribe he could make this killing process last for agonizing hours. Once dead, she too was tied up on the pyre for burning.

People from the crowd ran up to men already tied to the poles so they could "shave the New Christians." This meant setting their beards afire to provide an additional measure of agony. It was a common entertainment of the *auto-da-fés*. Then the effigies, dressed in *sanbenitos*, paraded around the *quemadero*. She might have known some of these people. Then came the bones, removed from their boxes, some advanced in decomposition, fresher ones still wearing moist mouldy skin and sinew, grinning green and horrible. Even the bones wore *sanbenitos* and miters. Then, one at a time—hundreds altogether—skeletons and effigies were hurled into the hungry fire.

This is what surrounded Maria, mother of my mothers, as she prepared to die: sparks erupted from the bonfire, the dying screamed, some about to die wept, others prayed. Priests pushed their pieties, and the crowd was wild with pleasure.

The executioner touched the brand to Maria's pyre. My

God, what could she have been thinking? In her place wouldn't I utter the magic words about Jesus Christ to save myself?

She did not. Why can't I say she was wrong? Even as I am about to watch her die I envy the power of her faith, and I look inside myself, wondering.

I called Dr. Elliot at Mt. Sinai hospital and asked him exactly what happens when someone is burned at the stake. He said he hasn't covered an *auto-da-fé* since he was a resident. While cautioning that some speculation was involved, he said this:

It would depend largely upon the wind. If it was calm and the flames rose straight up, death would result from asphyxiation. This would occur before the body was actually burning in the flames.

I asked if this would be painful, and he said yes, terribly. But it would not last long. However, if the wind blew the fumes away from the victim, it would be altogether worse. The flesh of the legs would cook, just like a roast. The pain would be intolerable. When the flames reached the groin, with its concentration of nerves and blood vessels, the pain would be overpowering. As the groin heated and circulation diminished there, blood pressure in her body would fall. The faster the better, because when it fell below 70 she would no longer notice the pain. She might have a moment of relative calm, which some people experience just before they die. When her pressure hit 60, she would fall unconscious, and feel no more pain. And at the end: ashes.

When I got off the phone I lit a candle. I resolved to hold my hand in the flame for ten seconds, ten short seconds. The pain was excruciating. After five seconds I had to pull it away. I am weak.

Maria died the more horrible, wind-blown option. The notary records that her long black hair was flowing with the breeze, and the crowd cried that she was an evil, beautiful witch. She strained against her bindings, but she did not cry out. She was not admired for this; Jewish fortitude at the stake was interpreted as collusion with Satan, who numbed heretics'

159

bodies to the torments. If only Satan had appeared and taken them all! The torments lasted almost an hour! Mercy.

Finally she reached that moment of calm Dr Elliot spoke of and said this:—*Sh'ma Yisra'el, Adonai Eloheinu, Adonai Ekhad.*

The priest cursed her again. He was tired of hearing this from heretics.

Then she said:—Juan . . .

But that was all. Soon the flames took her. What was she about to say? Juan, I love you? Juan, I should have repented? Juan, I have found peace in our God? Juan, your weakness has murdered me? I'll never know. I don't think I'll ever get over this.

TODAY I WENT over the guest list. I keep worrying that I forgot somebody, and she'll hate me forever. Of course if I asked anybody now she would hate me for asking her so late. Why bother. Somehow I feel like I should keep doing these things.

I also looked over the seating plan for the reception. I spread around the people who are going to get roaring drunk. If they want to start trouble, they'll have to travel to get together, but after a while they won't be able to get out of their chairs.

The only thing that didn't seem right was the head table. Everyone is in pairs except for Mrs. Beneviste. That would be OK if she was a maiden aunt. But Mrs. Beneviste will be the best looking woman at the table. She'll be the best looking woman in the whole reception, and she's going to get a lot of attention. My cousins, the Hot Young Things, usually own family gatherings, but they won't this time, and they won't want anything to do with her. They'll look at her and try to find something wrong with her. Good luck. I already tried that.

I saw Solly for dinner. It was just like last time we got together after we were kinky—we didn't talk about it. Maybe that's part of being kinky. I've been thinking about it all day. I keep reaching up for my cheek, thinking everybody can see it and they know exactly what happened! I made some amazing goofs at work today. And speaking of which, Peter stopped at my desk and asked me where we're going on our honeymoon—which is the first decent thing he's said to me in two months. I said I didn't know, and I am really looking forward to finishing up the on-line project when I get back. He said good, it will be waiting for me. So I was doing all this worrying about nothing. I guess I'll have to find something else to worry about now.

Anyway, I asked Solly if his mother was going to bring someone to the wedding. I didn't say "date." More like "prince." He said that she hasn't said anything about it. He would be very surprised if she wanted to bring somebody he hasn't met.

I said, "There has to be someone in her life."

"I don't know what goes on in her private life. We don't discuss it."

I thought they discuss everything, so this was a relief. I said, "But there have to be men. She's so, you know, sensual."

He made a weird face. "That's her business."

"I always figured she'd be breaking hearts left and right."

"Careful."

I let it go. He was looking out the window. Then he started talking in a soft voice. "I have never seen my mother with a man, in a romantic way, since my father died. Men approach her all the time, it's true, but she dismisses them. That's the way it's always been."

"But why?"

"I guess what I should say is that she dismisses them whenever I am around. I have no idea what she does on her own."

"You don't think she'd hide that from you?"

"I don't know. Now that you bring it up, I realize that all kinds of things could be happening, and I wouldn't know anything about them. She certainly is a beautiful and passionate woman to spend her years alone."

"Yes, she is."

"Maybe it's because of my dad. Maybe she's true to his memory. Or maybe she's true to my memory of him. I hope she hasn't given anything up because of me. I could never forget him."

"You loved your dad?"

"Oh, yes. Dad was wonderful. He used to give me big wet kisses on the ear, the kind you keep hearing for about ten minutes after they're over. When he and Mama were embracing, they would let me push my way in between. I can remember the heat and the smells. It was intoxicating. Even now if I catch a whiff of anything like it, it sends me right back to the moment." He laughed a little. "I guess we all have an amazing memory for smells."

I was holding back my tears.

He said, "And the way he always looked at me. Kind of laughing, kind of serious."

"Because that's the way you are."

"And the way Mama looked at him, like he was the center of the world."

I was going to say: "Just the way she looks at you now." But I thought better of it. Suddenly he had a look on his face that I've never seen before. Tender, young, worry-free. If only I could make him feel this way.

I said, "What happened to your dad?"

He shrugged. "It was out of the blue. He was thirty-four years old, slender like me, never sick a day in his life. And he just died. A heart attack."

"Was he playing raquetball, or shoveling snow or something?"

"That's a good question. I know he was home. I remember the ambulance screaming up to the house. It was night, and I remember the blue and red lights flashing all over the houses across the street. But I don't know that he was doing anything in particular."

I hugged him. "It must have been awful."

"I was a kid. I didn't even get it for a while. I remember being excited because a lot of people were coming to the house to visit us."

"But your poor mother."

"She fell to pieces. They sent me off to stay with my aunt for a month. When I returned Mama wasn't much better. She spent most of the day in bed, weeping. I used to get in and hug her and tell her it was all right. It must have been strange, coming from a five-year-old. But, you know, she was a young woman, just in her early twenties."

I said, "Oh my God. She was younger than us!"

"And suddenly she was alone. That's when she started to dress in black. She's been doing it for twenty-five years. Maybe it's not so strange that she doesn't go out with men. What were her chances of finding a man who could equal Dad?"

I said, "He must have been an amazing guy. I wish he could be at our wedding."

Solly stared at me for a minute. Then he put his hands over his face. His body was shaking, and tears started dripping between his fingers.

"I'm sorry. I'm sorry," I said. I hugged him.

I kissed his fingers. He turned away. I pressed my face against his back. I could feel the heat of his pain. And I didn't know what to do about it.

163

HERE I AM AT Mt. Sinai hospital, and they only have this tissue paper that my pen shreds. Like that. I'll have to copy this over when I get home. Don't people write in hospitals any more? There is nothing else to do. I sit here in my flimsy gown, obviously designed for the delight of lecherous doctors. No wonder they don't leave me alone.

I feel so foolish about being here. I like to think of myself as a graceful person. It would probably suit the Pennybaker clan just fine if I was stuck here for six more days, until after the wedding. But I will go home today. If I could only find my clothes.

I am fuzzy on the end of the day, but I remember the beginning very clearly. I was eager for Solomon to pick me up. We hadn't had a chance to talk all week, and of course I had a lot to tell him. When he kissed me he took my hand and felt the coarseness over the burn on my palm. He asked what happened, and I said—It's an old scar. Very, very old.

As we drove to the stadium I told him all about Juan and Maria, their interrogations, trials, and punishment.

He said—I get the feeling that I am supposed to be drawing a conclusion from this.

—How could you not?

—What is it supposed to be?

—How about this: Jews who act like Christians are called swine, and are treated like swine, all the way to the slaughter.

—Mama, I'm not like you. I can't live under the weight of five hundred years of people I didn't know.

—You can hardly accuse me of living in the past. Until you asked me to begin this family history, I knew nothing about it.

—That's true. And now you're a fanatic.

—No. Now I'm no longer ignorant. I want you to share the condition.

—But Mama, why should the Portuguese Inquisition—I feel weird even saying that—why should it affect my life? My wedding? It's just like the blacks and their four hundred years of slavery, and the Indians being forced off their land. Yes, it's all bad. It's terrible. But it's over.

—So to you it's as if none of this ever happened.

—No. Not at all. I feel for all these people. I admire the ones you've been telling me about. I'm proud to be related to them. But they're not going to affect my wedding.

—I think they will.

—How?

—Because you've got to come to terms with them, even if you try to ignore them.

—I don't know what that means.

—The only difference between them and us is that they lived when hostilities toward us were overt. Let me tell you, if you tried to hold this wedding five hundred years ago, your choices wouldn't concern caterers and photographers. It would be life and death—yours.

—You could just as soon say that if I was getting married a really long time ago, I would be choosing between walking upright or having a tail.

—How can I make you understand? It's all still there. It's right under the surface.

—I think I understand. I just don't agree.

—If you truly have a feeling for our history, do something for me. For both of us. Honor the family. Have a rabbi at your service.

—It's too late. The service is all planned.

—That's no answer. All he has to do is show up. He comes fully accessorized.

—The Pennybakers would get upset.

—Not Allison.

—That's probably true. But Louise would. You know this. That's why you taunted her.

—If Allison doesn't object, and even if she does, you are entitled to make a small gesture to honor your own past. What are you afraid of?

—Mama, why is this happening now? Why didn't it happen

when I was thirteen? Or last year? Why did you find religion a week before my wedding?

—It's inconvenient, I know. But then again, Maria Beneviste thought it was pretty damned inconvenient to be born during the Inquisition.

—Again the Inquisition.

—Your wedding will be in a church. Every aspect of it is going to be Christian. Yet you are afraid even to suggest a rabbi because your mother-in-law-to-be, who has not hesitated to spray our family with the baldest bigotry, might be ashamed.

—That's right.

—That's exactly what the *marranos* did. I have to tell you, it didn't work out for them.

—In other words, if I look out for Louise's feelings, I'm a swine.

We drove a while without talking. I wanted to think about what he had said. Finally I said—I love this country. But there's one thing it doesn't have: history. Most Americans act as if they might have magically appeared here. They can recognize old movie stars, but not photos of their own ancestors. We're different this way. We go back thousands of years, and the past lives in us, or maybe on us, or through us. I can see you and me in the transcripts of those awful trials. Those tragic people wrestled with the same moral and historical issues the same messy way that we do, that my parents did, and their parents. That's what I've learned these last two months. If you give those up, if you break your ties and live on the safe Christian surface of your life, it would be a tragic loss, to me, to the family, but most of all to you.

—All right, Mama. I know these issues are real. I've thought about them. But why do they have to be decided at the wedding?

—At some point you have to declare. I know the wedding is the right time because of the way you resist it. Soon you'll be too comfortable to care.

—Don't worry, Mama. You're taking care of my being too comfortable.

We drove on. Then I said—Allison loves you for your Jewish qualities. Though I'm sure she's never thinks of them that way.

—Maybe so, Mama. But why does she have to know?

What happened afterward is hazier. When I try to reconstruct the afternoon in the ball park, my head starts to hurt. We got to the stadium and met the Pennybakers at the seats. There was a whole batch of them, with cousins and nephews and such, and they all looked very comfortable, with their green sunshades and sunglasses and tennis whites, and beers in hand.

I sat beside Louise. She had left an open seat for me, so I didn't have a choice. I shouldn't say that. I wanted to sit with her. I was very curious to meet her. She seemed rather surprised when I appeared. Did she think I wasn't going to show, that I would commit such an affront a week before the wedding?

Louise is a large, square, well-fed woman, like Allison not pretty but not homely either, but unlike Allison she has a suspicious and defensive air. This was apparent before I opened my mouth. Her hair is dyed blond and lacquered, and she dresses in Lacoste, but a bit too young. She would look a lot better if she were more comfortable being a mature woman. By way of greeting she handed me a beer with a smooth and unconscious cock of the wrist. I didn't want to offend her by not accepting. We chattered a bit about the drive over, the weather, the seats—everything except our children and their union in her church. She wasn't easy with me.

Allison was on my other side, Solomon next to her. She seemed particularly anxious that her mother and I should get along. I think we did, as well as we ever will.

Our seats were in the full afternoon sun. I made a mistake by not bringing a hat. I soon felt that I would wilt, and was desperate for a beverage. Because I was in the middle of a long row, beer was the only drink readily available, from a man who walked about screaming a strange approximation of the word. I don't normally drink beer, since it is bitter to my taste.

The center of the activity in the baseball game was the five-sided base in front of the high fence, where the umpire in the big black uniform stood. One after the other the batters came up to this little white altar and paused for some kind of preparatory ritual, kicking the dirt, or striking their feet with their bat. Then something quite shocking happened. A batter stood beside the base and made the sign of the cross on his breast. The one who followed him did the same. Two more did it in the following inning. Now I had something worthwhile to discuss with Louise.

She:—The only players who do that are Catholic. Look at the names. Martinez, Fernandez. Some of them don't even speak English.

I:—But you don't have to speak when you do it.

She:—That's true. Jesus's language is love.

I:—But Protestants don't do it?

She:—No.

(I wanted to hear the explanation for this, but she didn't offer.)

I:—Do the players think that Jesus cares who wins the game?

She:—Jesus loves all people and all they do. (Rather an unsatisfactory answer.) Even people who don't believe in Him.

I:—(Noted.) What if a batter crosses himself at the plate and then strikes out? Doesn't that shake his faith?

She:—With these young Latin players, that happens a lot. At least the batter knows that Jesus loves him even when he does strike out.

I:—Do you think the batter is asking to be loved if he strikes out, or is he praying to hit a home run?

She:—Life doesn't always go the way we want. You and I know that better than anyone. But it's nice that there's the love of Jesus regardless.

Just then there was a terrible noise on the field. A runner collided with the catcher with terrific impact. People in the stands jumped up, screaming and brandishing fists. Much of the language was completely filthy. There was real hatred. If there hadn't been a fence holding everyone in, I fear they

would have stormed the umpire and killed him. I watched
Allison and Louise, shrieking as belligerently as everyone else,
beer spilling from their upheld cans. I don't want to think that
they can be swept up in a mob. I want to think the Pennybakers
are people of courage and independence. I worry for my Solomon in their hands.

The game went on for a long time. Then there was a break,
and the players went into their little trenches. Out in the grass
there was a procession, of civilians, not of players, which
eventually extended all the way across the field. It was
accompanied on both sides by officials on horseback. The
people marched slowly, irregularly, one at a time, each holding
up a sign, which I was too far away to read. The crowd, which
had been relatively well-mannered since the collision incident,
again started to get excited. The Pennybakers were standing
and pointing, making alarming high-pitched sounds. At the
end of the parade the men on the horses backed everyone up
against the wall.

169

I believe that this is when it happened. The heat had pretty
much melted me into my chair, and my mind buzzed with
Louise's insouciant bigotry. But I wanted to remain part of the
outing. I had promised Solomon. As I stood up to watch
the parade my eye was struck by a dazzling reflection of the
hot summer light from something, maybe on a horse's saddle,
or a badge worn by one of the officers. Everything turned an
absolutely blinding white. I fell back into my seat. Now that
I couldn't see, the wild noises around me seemed ever louder,
and the vibrations of the wild mob traveled up from my feet
into my heart. It was terrifying. I covered my eyes with my
hands, and slowly my vision faded from white to gray to black.

And then I knew what it was to participate in the greatest
of all Christian rituals—the *auto-da-fé*.

Without my vision I was a prisoner in my seat. Everyone
else was up, screaming at the parade. Why had I stayed? The
priests had come forward and crossed themselves with one
hand while they held bludgeons with the other. Was this not
bald enough for me? The loudspeakers began to crackle and

echo, and I couldn't make out a word. But I knew what they were announcing: the sentences of the marchers. The black-clad man standing beside the priests and controlling everything was obviously the magistrate of all destinies—the Inquisitor.

Though I had seen the prisoners—I mean the penitents—for just a moment, I could now recall them in detail. They were small, almost childlike, ragged, struggling under the weight of their placards. They were guilty of the unforgivable: they refused to cross themselves in front of the judge, they washed on Saturdays, they honored the god of Moses, the god of their parents. I am one of them, and it was only a matter of time until they came for me. With the eyes and ears of all my neighbors, including my new extended family, in their service, I had no chance to escape.

The cheering was so loud and prolonged that I could only conclude that the *auto-da-fé* had moved to its next phase—punishment. I couldn't hear the crack of leather yet, the splitting of flesh. I imagined the penitents were still being stripped down and mounted on their donkeys. The son of God was not served unless these people were first humiliated in their nakedness.

Still no sound of the switch. Perhaps the penitents were already being led away. I reached over to the chair where Solomon had been sitting. He was not there. They had him! He could be en route to the dungeon, where he would be left to rot. Or pulling on the massive oar of a warship while the executioner plied him with a cat-o'-nine-tails. How long could my soft-handed accountant last? The cheers around me continued unabated, drowning out my call of his name. If he was gone, I wanted them to take me too.

Still more horrible: Some of those people parading across the grass might be officials, carrying placards identifying effigies and boxes of bones. In one of the boxes was the body of my beloved Aaron, dug up after twenty-five years in the ground. They would stick a yellow fool's cap on his skull and parade him around like a grotesque marionette, and then cast him into the pyre.

Was this truly happening? I forced myself to open my eyes, to light that was once again blinding. But soon I could make out silhouettes. And then I saw that they were lighting the pyre right in front of the penitents! It was real!

I struggled to my feet. I was not going to let them take my son. I would find him.

Just then I heard a familiar whoop. And there he was, just a few feet away from me, standing like the others, taunting the people, living and dead, about to be incinerated in St. John's fire.

This was the darkest moment of my life. Christianity had taken my son. His soul is gone. He has become the kind of *marrano* who laughs at the torment of its victims. No wonder he wants to be married in a church.

I knew then that should I ever have to make the choice, I would choose the stake before the cross. I want Solomon to think the same way.

I called to him, or tried to. Horror closed my throat. That's all I remember. I must have fallen.

I woke up here, in this flimsy gown, with a bandage over the egg growing from my forehead. It is now apparent that I was dehydrated by the extreme heat—I sat in it for over three hours—and finally lost consciousness. I know it was just a ballgame and not an *auto-da-fé*. But that doesn't matter.

What's important is that I now know Christian fury, stripped of its modern apologetic presentation, the soothing words of its liberal clergymen. I can finally see the toll it is taking on the bond between my son and me. As I have suspected all along, the question as to which little building the wedding should be held in is trivial. The real issue is vast. I'm grateful to Louise for helping me see this. She and I have less than a week to do something about it.

Solomon and Allison just came in. I don't know if I'll ever be able to explain myself to him, and I just couldn't face her, since for all this I am still very fond of her. I held my head and told them I was sorry but I could not speak. They talked to the doctor and left. Since they will expect me to stay here a few days, I will leave this afternoon, by cab. That will gain me a little time alone, to continue my work. But I must say, my head hurts in a way I've never felt. I have to stop writing.

DISASTER! Mrs. Beneviste is in the hospital. She might not make it to the wedding, and now I realize I really want her there. What a world.

What a scene. We were at the ballpark, and Mother saw Solly and Mrs. Beneviste before they saw us. She asked who the beautiful young woman was with him. Did I know her, or was this someone out of his past? Insinuating that he was cheating on me. OK, Mother. I was going to tell her that Solly could never leave somebody who gives him such kinky sex. But this was even better—I just told her who Miriam was. Mother was furious! Spitting furious! I always thought that eventually you accept your lot and stop hating the beautiful ones. I guess not. Jeffrey kept buzzing around her. I don't think she even noticed him. He wants me to set him up with her. I should do it. That would certainly take Mother's mind off my wedding!

The problem was the heat. Mrs. Beneviste was wearing black, as usual. She didn't have a hat and we were in the sun the whole game. Mother offered her a beer when she sat down, and she kept drinking them all afternoon. Beer goes right to your head when you're sweating, even if you're seasoned like Mother and Dad. Mrs. Beneviste is not a drinker. She must have gotten dead drunk. But she's so polished that she didn't come across that way at all.

173

I overheard a really strange conversation she was having with Mother. It was about why the players were crossing themselves at the plate. Mrs. Beneviste was saying things like, "What if the batter and the pitcher both cross themselves? How does Jesus know who to choose?" Mother was pretty patient for a while. Then she started acting like a snooty church official. I stayed out of it. I was afraid they were going to break into the rabbi-in-the-church argument. But that didn't happen. I think Mother realized who she was up against.

Then Mrs. Beneviste leaned over to Solly and said, "They strike out and then retire in safety. Strikeouts should carry some real penalty. Scourging, or the galleys. Maybe even the stake. That would certainly make the game more interesting, and more deserving of Jesus's time."

Solly tried to take the beer from her. Mother gave me one of those looks, like it was my fault. Of course.

Mrs. Beneviste settled down for a while. But then there was a play that upset her. Glen Swieznicki tagged up from third on a short fly ball. The ump called him out at the plate, but he was safe. Of course the crowd got all upset. You don't just go calling Glen out like that! He's too handsome! Poor Mrs. Beneviste looked like she thought a riot was breaking out.

During the seventh inning stretch, they had the Banner Day parade in the outfield. Cousins Joey and Edward were in it, and we were all standing and clapping for them. This is when I started worrying about Mrs. Beneviste. She was sitting there with her hands over her eyes, muttering.

Finally they brought the winning banner up (not the cousins, though it should have been). They have a big horse shoe with Roman candles attached to it. The kid walked through and they set them off. Rockets were going off every which way.

174

That's when Mrs. Beneviste got up. She gave out a little scream and fell straight over. She smashed her head on cousin Ernie's chair, and she was out. Solly scooped her up like she weighed nothing. He ran down the stairway to the ambulance, which is always at the stadium during games. At the hospital the doctor said that nothing's broken, but they want to hold her. Head wounds are tricky. You don't know what can happen. Could there be a worse diagnosis?

OFFICE OF MEDICAL EXAMINER

BFI Job Number 62—4013
Chemist/technician: S. Benjamin
Examination of human cranium

1. Cranium is completely charred from fire. Left
zygomatic arch and left parietal bones are charred
to point of disintegration.
2. All cranial bones are without injury.
3. There is no evidence of soft tissue, hair, or
blood.

4. Microscopic samples were taken from
occipital, left and right parietal, frontal, and
left and right temporal bones. There was no
evidence of blood or marrow in the diploic space
of the flat bones.
5. Chemical analysis of surface of skull reveals
presence of shellac.
6. Remarks: If the cranium had been alive at the
time of subjection to high temperatures of a fire,
one would expect to find evidence of burned marrow
and blood in microscopic examination of the flat
bones. This cranium's lack of such indicates that
it was extremely dry, and thus old—deceased—long
before it was subjected to fire, perhaps 20—50
years before. The cranium shows remnants of
coating with shellac. This substance, long out
of general use (now replaced by cheaper
varnishes), was once sometimes used to preserve

bones. This cranium might have been used as an artifact. It was not a casualty of the fire on June 14.

I HAD TO STAY in the hospital an extra day. Doctor Elliot wanted me to stay longer, and I demanded an explanation. He said that I was not unconscious for very long, and that was good. But there was no way to know if I had suffered any local damage to my brain except to keep a watch of me. I said, after all those machines you put me on? He said that they can't always detect it. That's why we have to be careful. I said, what are you expecting me to do, drop dead? Tell me. I don't want to ruin any good clothes when I fall. He said, there's no way to predict. Some people become lethargic and lose interest in things. Others do just the opposite. They get energetic, impulsive, and uninhibited. He said that it can be very destructive. I said I'd watch for any changes in myself. He said that that wasn't really possible, since no one can judge her own judgement, even someone as exceptional as me. I grabbed him and kissed him on the mouth and told him I'll be careful. He turned as red as a pomegranate. When I insisted on leaving, he made me promise to come back in two days. I don't see the point. What more will he know then? It is just a pretext to see me again.

This is a very busy week. I have to understand—to master— and to act. This is the question: Why would the Jews convert to Christianity in the first place? *Marranos* met with great worldly success, but at the price of the hatred of their countrymen and then becoming fodder for the Inquisition. Why would anyone strike such a deadly bargain?

Reading has never given me such a headache. It must be the tension of discovery. I took two pills that Doctor Elliot gave me, but they did nothing. So much for modern medicine.

1492. All Jews were expelled from Spain, hundreds of thousands of them. The Benevistes, who started there, went to Portugal. According to the genealogy thoughtfully provided to me by the Inquisitor, Eva and Isadore Beneviste arrived in Lisbon in December 1492 with seven children. They came by foot, over the mountains, a brutal trek which buried many. Though the Jews were forced to leave all their wealth behind in Spain, Isadore was able to pay the entrance fee, levied by the King Joao II of Portugal. Had he not, the family would have become slaves of the Portuguese crown. Slaves!

King Joao died in 1495. His successor, King Manoel, wanted to marry Isabel, daughter of Ferdinand the Catholic and Isabella the Catholic of Spain—the very rulers who brought the Inquisition to the Iberian Peninsula. Isabel refused to enter Portugal until it was cleansed of infidels. And so in December 1496, all Jews and Moslems were given until the following October to leave the country, or die. But have a nice day.

178

Eva and Isadore and the others prepared for departure, just as they had in Spain five years earlier. But King Manoel, unlike Ferdinand, realized that the country would suffer if the immense Jewish talent and wealth left the country. This expulsion was no expulsion at all. It was a mass forced conversion. These pills are useless. I'm going to try Tylenol with codeine.

When the deadline for departure approached, Manoel summoned the Jews to Lisbon to board ships for foreign asylum. But there were no ships. Upward of twenty thousand Jews were packed into the Os Estaos palace and deprived of food and drink.

Then the ultimate cruelty: the king had his soldiers take the children. They, and all Jewish children, were forcibly baptised—even though Jesus says that forcible baptism is a violation of the soul. Why didn't Jesus show up in Portugal? Maybe if he didn't have all those baseball games.

The parents could reclaim their new Christian children (with their new Christian names) if they themselves were baptised. Most of the children of parents who refused baptism were distributed throughout Portugal, as far as possible from their parents, to be brought up as Christians by Christian families. Seven hundred of them had an even grimmer fate. They were shipped to the uninhabitable island of Sao Tome off the African coast, where most soon died of disease or were eaten by crocodiles. Helpless children eaten by cold-blooded reptiles!

The deadline for departure from Portugal passed. Now the Jews, including the ones still locked up in the palace, were considered to be in the country illegally. Therefore they had no rights, no possessions. They were all King Manoel's slaves. This broke Eva and Isadore Beneviste, and most of the remaining holdouts. They accepted baptism. They became swine.

This is the moment I have been searching for: the first time the Beneviste family accepted Christ. Imprisoned, starved, stripped of our children, and now, by virtue of the king's deception, his slaves. After all my studies, I recognize this face of Christian love.

Eva and Isadore were reunited with three of their children, now named Juan and Maria (probably the Beneviste family's first) and Isabel. Their other four children, who they never saw again, had already been given away to Christian families. Possibly these four lost children, and certainly their children, never knew that they were scions of Abraham. But they and their descendants would always be swine in the eyes of the church.

I would choose sacrifice instead. But could I sacrifice my child? The idea makes my head feel as if it will explode all over my living room. When will this feeling pass? There is a wedding on Saturday.

I SAW MRS. Beneviste at the hospital. She has a bump on her head, but that's about it. From the sound her head made hitting that seat I thought it would be much worse. It helps that she has that beautiful skin. If it was me, I would look like I was wearing an eggplant. Solly stayed with her.

When I got to Mother's, she acted very worried. Is Miriam all right? Was she badly hurt? Will she be at the wedding? When I said yes to that, it was the end of the concern.

Then Mother insisted on knowing when Solly and I are going for our last class with Father Phillips. I told her that we've had our last class.

She said, "Really. Some people spend their lives studying the words of Jesus and go to the grave wishing they had had more time, just so they could have studied them some more."

I said, "That's not my ambition in life."

She said, "How can you be sure if you don't know what he has to say?"

"The last meeting was supposed to be about sex. OK? Do you want us to be thinking about sex any more than we already are?"

"I am not a prude, dear. I know that may surprise you." It did surprise me, because she is a prude and she said it just like a prude. "And neither is Jesus. He does not ask you not to think about sex. He asks that you do it in the proper way."

"Come on, Mother. On your wedding night, how much time did you spend thinking about Jesus?"

I stepped over her body and tucked my smoking pistol back into the holster. I have to go see Solly now. I hope he's not too bummed out.

I'm looking back over this. I wrote it maybe five hours ago, and it's ancient history. Mrs. Beneviste is going to drive me straight from the wedding chapel to the funeral parlor. If I don't get this down on paper, I'm never going to believe it.

Solly was worried. He said that Doctor Elliot told him that these injuries to the front of the head can change people. It's called frontal syndrome. She could act out in ways locked up inside her but that we never see. A bigger-than-life Miriam Beneviste. A scary thought. But Doctor Elliot said there was no telling when it would happen, or if something else altogether would happen, or if nothing would. He had already seen a few disturbing signs. We have to watch her. If she changed at all she would deny it. There was no use arguing with her. He wants her to stay in the hospital for a few more days, but he doesn't think she will. She said she has a lot to do before the wedding. I thought, like what? Now I know. Put her back in.

At Solly's place he talked and talked about his mother. He didn't want to eat because he was too upset. But finally he got hungry and we had some dinner. The food helped.

But when I touched him, he jumped away. People don't do that when they're just nervous. I decided I'm not going through that again, not during the last week before the wedding. I need him now.

After dinner I held his hand while we watched some TV. Then I did a little kissing and rubbing. I couldn't tell what he was thinking. I asked him if he wanted to mess around.

He said, "Not with my mother in the hospital!"

I said, "What's that got to do with it?"

"It wouldn't be right. It would be disrespectful."

"Disrespectful? What are you, a Catholic all of a sudden?"

"She's lying there with her head mashed in, and I would be here, you know."

"First of all, her head is not mashed in. She has a bump. She is probably going home tomorrow. I bet she would be happier if she knew you were taking care of me. That's what she would be doing in the same situation."

"It doesn't feel right. I'm sorry."

We sat there for a while, and I was getting mad. I wasn't going to let her take him away from me. Again. In yet another way. I said, "You know, the last two times we made love were after you hit me."

He jumped. "Shh. Don't say that."

"What's going on? Now I can't talk here either?"

"I don't like to hear you say that."

"But it's true. Now if you want, I could pull open this scab again,

181

and you could hit me, and then you would make love to me like a madman." I couldn't believe I was saying this. Now he was really getting nervous. His neck was as stiff as a light pole.

I said, "Or we could try it like regular people. I'll tell you what, let me start. If you don't like it, we'll forget it. OK? You let me know."

He didn't say anything. So I pulled down his zipper and started to do my thing. My big friend was up in a flash. I guess it wasn't worried about Miriam. Soon I could feel Solly's fingers pushing through my hair.

And then, bingo. The door opened. The front door of his apartment. There she was, about six feet away. Miriam Beneviste.

Well, I had an interesting decision to make. Do I continue to hide his thing in my mouth, which would make me look like my face was attached to the front of his pants? Or do I pull off it, and let it stick straight out for his mother to see?

Solly tried to scream something, but his voice cracked. He tried again. "Mother, what the hell are you doing here? What are you doing?"

I could feel his thing drooping and rolling up. It took about one second. I let it slip out, and tried to sit so I was in between it and Miriam. She wasn't embarrassed at all.

Solly said, "I thought you were still in the hospital."

She said, "I had your keys. I wanted to talk to both of you."

"Couldn't you ring the bell?"

"I didn't want you to prepare for me."

He turned away and zipped himself up. I never saw sweat show up so fast. My heart was pounding. But at least my clothes were on. I'd hate for her to see me naked.

He had a stronger voice now that his pants were closed. He said, "We'll talk some other time, Mama. I think you should leave. This is outrageous. And leave the keys here."

"I have every right to be here."

"You do? Since when?"

"During the Inquisition, the Dominicans had the right to enter and search any Jewish home at any time."

"The Dominicans? What are you talking about?"

"With your wedding coming, I want you to understand the religious issue. You should hear this too, Allison. You think I've been telling you faraway stories about faraway people. But they were Benevistes, just like you and me. If this was the Inquisition, I could ransack this place, and if I found one incriminating shred, like a book I didn't approve, I could throw you in a dungeon indefinitely, confiscate everything you own, torture you, and maybe even burn you to death."

Solly stared at her. "Are you feeling all right?"

"The church considers you a swine, Solomon. And why not? Your tribe introduced the sins of Sodom into the world, and contaminated the Christians—just as you were doing when I came in. You can hardly blame them for wanting you dead."

I wanted to run and hide. But I couldn't let her do that to me. "I go to church, Mrs. Beneviste. The priest never says anything bad about Jews. Never."

"I'm afraid, my dear, that even when the devil is not mentioned, he never loses his tail."

Solly said, "And just who is the devil?"

"You and I are, my son. Well, I'm going now. I wanted you two to feel a moment of fear of the blood and the fury of the church and the temple."

And bingo, she was gone!

After a few minutes of silent shock, Solly said, "I have to call Doctor Elliot."

"Why?"

"It's frontal syndrome. I have to tell him."

"How do you get that?"

"She is completely out of control. Just as he warned."

I said, "I think she is completely in control."

"Then why would she do this?"

"To strike fear into the heart of your fiancée. She did a great job."

"Never. She would never do anything this crazy if she was well."

"Solly! Wake up! This has been coming for months. She doesn't want to lose her son."

"I don't believe it. She would never do this."

We'll see. If he ever gets hard again, which will be a miracle, maybe I'll believe him.

JOAO III, King Manuel's successor, married Catalina, a grand-daughter of Ferdinand and Isabella. This ambitious woman brought the Inquisition to Portugal, even though Judaism had long been outlawed and Jews were persecuted without any help from the Vatican.

And it was Isabel, Ferdinand and Isabella's daughter, who first insisted that all Jews leave Portugal.

What poisoned the hearts of Ferdinand and Isabella?

The young Isabella, newly Queen of Castile, was quite taken with the handsome (and, apparently, partly Jewish) Ferdinand of Aragon, but there was strong opposition to him at court. The courtier Pedro de la Cavalleria had great success on Ferdinand's behalf, and provided the fabulous pearl collar that Ferdinand gave Isabella as his pledge. Don Abraham Seneor, the chief tax collector of Castile, sent for Ferdinand, whose friend Jaime Ram paid for the journey. In peasant disguise Ferdinand crossed the frontier to Seneor's home in the middle of the night. Seneor took him to marry Isabella at a fortress Seneor had secured for them.

185

Such a romantic story! Except for this: Seneor was the chief rabbi of Castile, Ram was the son of a famous rabbi, and de la Cavalleria belonged to a notable *marrano* family. Within twenty-five years these monarchs expelled all Jews from their land. Swine, thy name is Ferdinand and Isabella.

The two filled their court with Jews and *marranos*. Ferdinand's court confidant was a Jew, as was the commander of the fleet, and the court treasurer. Queen Isabella's confessor was a *marrano*. And here's one for Louise Pennybaker: Ferdinand the Catholic's cup-bearer was Jewish.

Ferdinand's interest was money—he was waging a long war against the Moors, and the treasury was empty. The Inquisition confiscated the estate of everyone it arrested. When the Jews were expelled, they were forced to leave their property and valuables behind.

Isabella the Catholic cared only that her domain was cleansed of the sin of heresy, a promise she had made to her childhood confessor. That man, like Ferdinand of mixed blood, was Tomas de Torquemada, later the bloody Grand Inquisitor of Spain.

How did Isabella, Isabel, and Catalina come to love Jesus so dearly and then slaughter scores of thousands of his tribesmen? I cannot answer this. Nor why men of mixed blood turn against their Jewish portion so savagely. But this is a compelling reason not to produce one in our family.

These were by no means the only bloody females in Spain and Portugal. Women regularly led mobs into Jewish quarters for mayhem and massacre. It was also women who were more likely to resist them, to refuse to betray their faith, and to die at the stake.

It is shocking, painful to think of women being so bloodthirsty. Then again, I cannot compare the strength of Solomon's resolve to mine, or even to Allison's. I dropped in on them last night, and she had him under control in classic fashion. Louise Pennybaker's husband, whose name I can't remember, is completely eclipsed by the strength of his wife. I have been wasting my time dealing with Solomon on the issue of faith. It will be decided by women. I should have realized this from the beginning.

THREE DAYS TO GO. I can barely eat I'm so nervous. It's not about getting married, or the wedding, or Solly. It's Mrs. Beneviste. She will do anything.

I wanted Solly to talk to her, but I knew he wouldn't. He's just like Jeffrey, a big strong man who's afraid of his mom. I knew I had to do it myself. Though I was hoping to break out in gigantic hives so I had an excuse not to.

When I knocked on her door she didn't seem surprised to see me. She asked me in and made some tea. I couldn't drink it.

She said, "So, Allison, tell me why you have come."

I said, "Solly really loves you, Mrs. Beneviste. He absolutely adores you."

She nodded. Yes. What else is new?

I said, "He would never do anything to hurt you."

"Not intentionally."

"Never. This wedding is so strange. People are getting all worked up when we just want them to be happy that we're getting married."

She stood up. I couldn't help thinking she was trying to intimidate me with her body. It worked, of course.

She said, "I think you are a fine young woman, Allison. You are a good match for my son. The only problem is religion. Doesn't your mother feel the same way?"

I wasn't going to let her drag Louise into this. "But neither one of us is very religious. We respect each other's feelings. I can't imagine that religion would ever be a problem."

"How are you going to raise your children?"

"Well, we haven't discussed it. But I know we will expose them to both religions. Both have so much to offer."

"And then the children are supposed to choose among them?"

"Yes."

"Between Mommy's religion and Daddy's religion?"

"It won't be like that."

"Between AC and DC? Between hot-blooded and cold-blooded?"

"I don't know what you mean."

"I mean religion isn't a choice, especially for a child. It's basic to the way you function. It's in your blood, your language, your identity. You can't just expect a child to choose one and have everything fall into place."

I remembered Louise saying basically the same thing. She used the aspirin analogy. I could have used an aspirin right then.

I said, "I don't know what to say to you. What can we do? How can we save the wedding?"

She said, "Maybe you can tell me, Allison. As you know, I've been looking into the history of our family, and what I've found is hundreds of years of vicious persecution at the hands of the Church for nothing more than a difference of faith. How should I feel about my son being married in one such church? How would you feel?"

"But that was the Catholic Church!"

"The Christian church. The name of the sect is of no interest to the people on the other end of its lash."

There was no sense trying to explain our denomination. I said, "I understand the way you feel. But you can't judge all Christians by the fanatics. I would go to the wall for Solly. I swear I would."

"Maybe you would. But that doesn't matter."

"Why?" I felt tears about ready to run.

"Because you do not run the world. I'm sure we would all be better off if you did."

"I don't want to run the world. I just want to love Solly and take care of him. What can I do? Please."

She sat down next to me. Here it was. "If you are as flexible about religion as you say, if you truly have regard for my concerns, this is what I suggest. Convert to Judaism. Be married in a synagogue by a rabbi. Join Solomon in his faith, and come to terms with the behavior of the Church toward your new religion."

I began to cry. She caught me completely by surprise, and everything came crashing down. Because all this time I was on Solly's side, and her side, and I was furious with Mother for all the holy crap she was trying to put us through. And I wanted the rabbi. I could picture him right there in the church. But now Mrs. Bene-viste called my hand. I realized that I don't want to postpone the wedding. I want to be married Saturday. And it has to be at my church. I've wanted it all my life, and it matters very much to me. But even more than that, I can't be Jewish. I just can't. I'm Christian—whatever that means. It's in my blood, like she said, and it always will be. Even though that feels like it's going to ruin everything.

Mrs. Beneviste held my hand and let me cry. I didn't want to tell her the truth, because I was afraid of what she would say. So I said, "But my mother. It's her church. She would be so upset!"

Mrs. Beneviste looked at me. She wasn't surprised at all. She smiled a little and said, "This is probably the first time you have the very slightest idea of how I feel about the wedding."

She was right. I am lost.

I GOT SOME interesting mail today, a survey of the Rogers families of the seaports of southern England. I ordered it over a month and a half ago—after factoring out the inflation in Louise's story about the role of her family members crossing the ocean—then completely forgot about it in all the excitement from Portugal.

Allison stopped over tonight for a little chat. She is a nice young woman, and she loves my Solomon, but she has no idea of how complex this wedding is. I can't provide her with a sense of history. She simply doesn't have it. So I have nothing to appeal to, no parallels to draw for her. She probably thinks I'm a crotchety old woman bent on nothing but trouble. Maybe I am. But it's more than that. And I am bent on it.

Solomon left work to stop at the library and tell me I had an appointment with Doctor Elliot today, which I had not made. He scheduled it for my lunch hour. He practically begged me to go. Why? Because of a headache now and then? It's ridiculous. To humor him, I went. I can't help suspecting that he and the Pennybakers are hoping that it will keep me from the wedding. No bars could hold me.

Doctor Elliot was terribly solicitous, with all his silly questions and little tests. I'm sure I passed everything at a walk. He picked up a skull and took the top off. I asked him if it was real. He said this one was a plastic casting, but the others in the case were real. This one would do for our purposes.

Then he showed me what he is worried about. The brain is cushioned, but it can move and twist on impact. There is no telling whether there is any minor local damage, and it is important not to aggravate it. He wouldn't feel confident about me for a little while longer.

I said—In other words, you want to see me again.

—Yes. In a few days.

—You find me attractive, don't you?

—Yes. But that's not why I am asking you to return.

—Are you sure?

—I don't want you to take this problem too lightly.

—Which problem? Yours or mine?

—You seem quite aggressive today.

—I just want to know the truth about your interest in me.

—Why?

—If I believe you I would be more inclined to believe your diagnosis about my frontal lobe.

—Wait here. I am going to get something you should read.

When he left the room I looked into the glass case. It held six skulls, each with a tag, a placard. That gave me an idea. I slipped one of the skulls into my bag. I will return it at my next appointment. How about that. I'm volunteering to come back.

He returned and gave me a copy of an article. Maybe I'll find time to read it. I didn't kiss him this time as I left. Let him think about which way he likes better.

I DON'T KNOW what to write. Here I am. The wedding rehearsal is tomorrow. I'm a wreck. My friends say, Don't worry. Everybody feels that way. It's only natural—Yeah, sure. If they only knew. This isn't natural.

I haven't seen Solly in a couple of days. We agreed to wait until the rehearsal, and now I'm really glad. I feel like I'm totally letting him down by not converting and doing it his mother's way. But I know I couldn't do it. It wouldn't be right. I'm sure she's going to tell him what happened. Is he going to hate me? Does he care? How did I get so far knowing nothing about this?

Some of the cousins are coming in tonight. It's going to be good to see them. They'll help me get my mind off the Inquisition. God, I hope I never hear that word again as long as I live.

I just filled out the forms to change my name. Visa card, driver's license, social security card, bank card. I'm turning into a new person. Allison Beneviste. I've wanted this name for so long! But now I can only think about all the horror the Beneviste name went through all these years. What kind of wedding is this?

Ignore what I just wrote. I'm nervous. Everything is going to be fine. I know it. I'm two days from the greatest day of my life. I'm marrying the man of my dreams. Everything will be fine. I know it.

THOUGH WE WEREN'T due at the church until afternoon, Solomon stopped by during the morning. He looked terribly handsome.

I said—The day before your wedding. How does it feel?

—I'm nervous.

—I've never known a groom to go calmly down the aisle. Not even your father.

—It's not that, Mama. It's you.

—I feel fine. I told you. I didn't even need to take a pill this morning.

—I mean your attitude about the church. I understand it. But the fact is that I am marrying a Christian and I am doing it in a church. Whatever you have to say about that, say it now.

—All right. You should not repeat the mistake of the *marranos*. If you must go into that church, bring your faith with you.

—I am bringing it with me. I bring it everywhere I go.

—That's facile, dear. Bring it and show it, in the person of a rabbi. There is still time to arrange it. I know a good man for the job.

—No, Mama. It wouldn't mean the same to me as it does to you.

—There you're wrong. Someday you'll know it. But if not for yourself, do it for me, just as Allison is doing it for Louise.

—Allison is doing it for herself. She goes to church. I will honor you in ways that have meaning for me. I don't have to make a stand in the church.

—You can't imagine how much this hurts me. And you won't know until you have a child who does it to you. Heaven forbid.

—Don't do this to me, Mama. Don't make me choose. Let's agree to disagree.

—I am not the one making you choose. The world makes you choose. When you walk down the aisle of that church you are choosing.

—I am choosing to have my wedding in a church. That's

193

all. I am above all your son and I will always be your son. I need your blessing. Privately, between us. It's the most important thing in the world to me.

I've never seen him so earnest, so passionate, so adult.

I said—Now you're making me choose.

—I hope you don't feel it's much of a contest.

—I love you more than the world. And I think you are making an error that could follow you all of your days. How can I combine those two so that it sounds like a blessing?

He took my hand—Let me tell you something. I love Allison. I want to spend my life with her. I love her in the way that you loved Dad.

—What do you know about that?

—What do I know about it? It made me what I am. It lives in me.

I looked at him, and I could see Aaron all over him. He said—I've thought about the idea of this marriage every way I can. I've felt its love, measured its risk. I've watched our engagement endure several difficult trials. I have considered the news of the family past from you. This is an examined love.

—So?

—It's the fundamental way Jews see the world: The commentary. The examination. The process as important as the text. You told me that.

—I still don't see what you're trying to tell me.

—I'm trying to tell you that I have done everything just as you would want me to.

—Except for the Christian part.

—Like it or not I have agreed to marry Allison. I have a duty to her. Even if everything were to come apart tonight, I have a sacred responsibility to her.

—You already feel that she's become a duty? A responsibility?

—It's a duty I do happily, willingly. You see, Mama, that in spite of yourself you have raised a son driven by Jewish values. I will go through with the wedding because, among many other reasons, there is no other just course. I don't think that you'd want me to walk out on her now. Even for you.

He was so commanding, so thoughtful, so handsome. It was as if Aaron had reappeared. I pressed him to me so I could feel his entire body, and I cried and gave him my blessing. Then I kissed him on the lips.

He struggled away—Come on, Mama.

—If you're man enough to speak like that, you shouldn't be afraid to kiss your mother.

Again I kissed him. He didn't resist this time. I could feel my heart tripping along irregularly, like a runner who was badly out of shape.

I can give him to Allison, because she will never displace me from the center of his heart.

I'M GOING TO change the front of this diary to "Allison Pennybakers's Believe It Or Not." It's the night before my wedding, but I don't know if I'm getting married. I don't think I'm going to find out until I'm standing at the altar in front of Father Phillips. We're going to find out together. Won't that be fun.

When Solly picked me up I thought the day was going to be golden. He was wearing his special wide-eyed smiley love look. It had been three days, but when he hugged me I knew I was safe.

We drove to the church. Mother and Dad were already there. Mother had that church look on her face, pink and happy, but she was watchful. This was her turf. Dad kind of followed after her.

Everybody started showing up: Jeffrey and Margaret, the bridesmaids, and the ushers. Trudy had an attitude. She's having trouble with Charles, and she doesn't want to think about people getting married. Too bad. Solomon wanted to know which one was Bonnie. He said, "You know what they say about the size of a woman's foot . . ." Whatever that means. Everyone was very chatty. I started feeling easier about the whole thing.

Father Phillips came in and told us what we were going to do. Could we start? I thought everybody was there. But I was wrong.

We were all walking toward our positions when the doors opened. I want to say that Miriam cast a shadow from there all the way to the altar. It just felt that way. Everybody turned around to look at her. She has that kind of power over people.

She slowly walked up the aisle. People cleared out of her way. She kissed me on the cheek, then she shook Mother's hand and asked where she should stand. I couldn't believe it! She had come into the church.

My attendants and Dad and I went into the lobby. Mrs. Cross started playing the procession music on the organ. Samantha the flower girl started down the aisle, then Steffy, Bonnie, Alice, Trudy, and Margaret. I watched through the window. When Dad and I made our entrance, he was trembling, so I held his hand really tight. He led me up to the front. He was almost crying, the sweet guy. I turned around to look at the church. I felt tears in my eyes. What a beautiful little building, with its white stone pillars and stained glass windows. I remember coming here when I was very small and it looked huge, like you could fit the whole world in it. I can mark so much of my life by events that happened right here. It is only right that I am getting married here. I looked at Solly. I am so grateful to him for this.

I looked at the first pew. On one side, pink and proud and ever watchful—Mother. On the other side, mysterious and beautiful and funereal—Miriam Beneviste. They were sitting maybe twenty feet apart, but the real distance was miles. Centuries. I had a pang of fear. But then I thought—why? She could have stopped the wedding several ways—such as cutting off the money—and she didn't.

Father Phillips said he would take us through a short version of the service. He had Solly and me face him and he said this:

"Dearly beloved. We have come together in the presence of God to witness and bless the joining together of this man and this woman in Holy Matrimony."

He said he would ask for anyone with objections to our marriage to speak now or forever hold their peace. I didn't dare turn around to look at Miriam. But she didn't say anything. I know it was just a rehearsal, but I took that as her consent. I was thrilled.

Next we take each other as husband and wife. Father Phillips said he would read a passage from Ephesians, which tells us to walk in love, as Christ loved us. And now the part that always makes me cry at other people's weddings: We face each other and Solly takes my hand and gives his solemn vow to stay with me from this day forward, until death do us part. Then I do the same. Father Phillips said not to worry, he would tell us our lines slowly. But that's one thing I could never ever forget.

Then he will ask the Lord to bless the rings. He asked if we're both wearing rings, and I assured him we were. We will put them on each other's fingers and Father Phillips will pronounce us husband and wife! "Those whom God has joined together let no one put asunder." And no one ever will! Or at least that's what I thought at that moment.

Father Phillips told Solly and me to kneel at the altar. He warned me that it might be a little harder to do that when I was in my dress. Solly might have to help me up.

I knelt. Solly looked down at me, right into my face, right into the center of my head. Then he smiled. And he knelt beside me. I kissed his shoulder.

Father Phillips said, "Most gracious God, we give you thanks for your tender love in sending Jesus Christ to come among us, to be born of a human mother, and to make the way of the cross to be the way of life."

I heard a voice behind me. "Get up!"

I thought it was a woman talking to her child.

Father Phillips continued. "By the power of your Holy Spirit, pour out the abundance of your blessing upon this man and this woman."

I heard the voice again. This time there was no mistaking it. It echoed through the church. "Get up, Solomon!" It was Miriam Beneviste.

Solly said to me, "Oh, no."

Father Phillips stopped his prayer and looked up. Miriam was standing in the center aisle, not far from him. She is not a large woman, but from where I was kneeling she looked huge and terrifying. Father Phillips did not say a word.

Solly did not get up. He looked back at her and said, "Sit down, Mama."

"Off your knees! We do not kneel!"

"This is not the time, Mother. We'll discuss it later."

"There will be no discussion on this subject. Get up!" From the rage in her voice, I would have gotten up myself if she asked.

Father Phillips looked at her, at him. There were no instructions in his little book for this. Everyone in the church was frozen. The place was silent.

Solly got up. He walked over to Miriam. He was furious. They talked in an intense whisper. I didn't dare go near them.

Then Solly turned and said, "I'm sorry, everyone. We're going to have to take a break for a few minutes."

Father Phillips nodded. Everybody hustled for the exits. I would have too, if it wasn't my wedding. I was still on my knees, begging for a miracle. When Mother started towards Solly and his mother, I saw that I wasn't going to get it. I got up and tried to stop her. She shook me off.

Mother said, "How dare you show such disrespect in a house of God."

Miriam turned to her and shook Solomon off the same way. "No son of mine will ever kneel to the cross, madam. I don't care whose house it is."

"Mrs. Beneviste, I warn you against such talk in front of the altar of His son."

"I deal directly with the Almighty, Mrs. Pennybaker."

"God's will is revealed through his son Jesus Christ. You people will continue to live in the wilderness until you realize it and accept him."

"Accept him, madam? Christian daggers have been letting my family's blood for five hundred years."

"What nonsense!"

"It may all be nonsense. The difference is that we don't torture and kill people to convert them to our nonsense."

"Jesus would never allow people to be brought into his church against their will."

"Maybe not. But many Christians would."

"You are outrageously insulting! I am asking you to leave my church and not return."

"Do you dare deny that you have exerted pressure on my son to join?"

Solly said, "She hasn't."

"Quiet!"

Mother said, "Your son has shown a lively interest in the church. He has attended classes here. He wants to join our family in Jesus."

"The Rogers family?"

"That is my maiden name."

"How would you feel if this proud Rogers family descended from a Jewish family which forsook their faith centuries ago?"

"I believe you are confusing my proud lineage with your lost one."

"What if your family Rogers used to be called Rodriguez, Jewish sailors from Spain, who emigrated to England during the Inquisition and changed their name and their faith?"

"I would say you were insane as well as insulting."

"What if the crucial difference between the Rogers and Beneviste families is that yours fled and gave up your God, while mine stayed and suffered the price of remaining true? What if your insistence on our kneeling is not holy at all, but is rather the need for company in your shame?"

Mother looked as if her eyes were going to fly out of her head. She said, "My good woman, I don't know what madness makes you speak this way to a licensed chalice bearer and lay reader of the Episcopal Church. Our lives are guided by the truth of Christianity."

"I am prepared to go on with the wedding of these two young swine. So long as we honor the moment when our families first fell to their knees, and when the Benevistes got back up."

"This is absolute sacrilege!"

"Don't worry, Mrs. Pennybaker. We will not think the less of you for your family's weakness."

"Leave now!"

"Isn't that what Jesus would say? Forgive you your weakness?"

"Don't utter his name! Don't you dare!" Mother was trembling now. I was afraid for her heart.

Mrs. Beneviste said, "Too bad Jesus is never in church when you need him."

Solomon left with his mother. I took Mother aside. I am absolutely lost.

I WENT TO THAT church fully intending to bless the wedding, as I told Solomon this morning. My heart was light, my mind clear. He looked terribly handsome, Allison looked lovely, the church was charming.

But I was a fool. How could I hope to escape the poison of the church right in its lair?

The priest made my son kneel before the cross, and I couldn't bear it. It was not an act of will on my part to speak aloud. My mind was overcome by images of the tortured Juan Beneviste kneeling before the Inquisitor's cross; of Eva Beneviste going to her knees after her seven children were stolen and dragged to the baptismal font; of the condemned women at the *auto-da-fé* of Maria Beneviste, who knelt to the cross only to receive the garrotte and the fire. How could I not speak?

Solomon challenged me in front of those people, which embarrassed me terribly. I never wanted them privy to the heart of our family. Then Louise did the same, and the exchange was not pleasant. Underlying it, as always, is the Christians' insistence that God is theirs exclusively, and that we heathens learn to accept his love their way, even if it kills us. I could not allow this arrogance to go unchallenged at my son's wedding.

Solomon said only one thing to me on the way home—Is it true about the Rogers family?

I told him it could well be—it was true of many families of that name from those places—but that to find out if the Pennybakers were among them would take more research, which I was quite certain they would never do. The risk was too great. I asked if he watched Louise's face when she first contemplated the possibility of Jewish blood in her body. She would have reacted with less horror if I told her she had AIDS.

I thought he might say that a wedding is one of those occasional havens from bloody history. But Louise may finally have made him see that history is seething all around him. He does not go alone to that altar. All the Benevistes go with him.

This is not easy for me. I grieve for his loss of Allison, who is a good and worthy woman. However, he will learn that he can live without her; I have survived twenty-five years without one of God's finest men. Solomon cannot endure without the freedom of his soul, which countless of his tribe have died trying to secure. Tomorrow I will convince him. Then we will put the matter behind us.

EVERYONE WANTED me to go out to dinner with them, but I had to wait for Solly. I was giving up hope when he finally showed up, after ten. I was never so glad to see anyone in my life! I hugged him and my tears poured out until I was dry. I must have been a sight.

I had to ask him why his horrible mother did that in the church. Everybody hated her for it, Mother most of all. Father Phillips talked to her for a long time, but he couldn't soothe her this time. She was still pale when I left the house.

And what about tomorrow? What is Miriam planning? She can stop the wedding all by herself. One woman standing in front of the altar dumping on Jesus Christ does the job. Now we know she's capable of it.

Solly said, "You can't imagine how sorry I am. I want to apologize to your mother."

"That's not a good idea. Not just yet."

"Is she still willing to go ahead with the wedding?"

"She said that she would let me marry you over her dead body. What do you expect? But she'll be fine tomorrow. What about your mother?"

"That is the question. I've never seen her like this. I should call Doctor Elliot."

"It won't do any good. She has him wrapped around her pinky." And I started to get really scared again. "Solly, what can we do?"

"You mean, do I still intend to marry you?"

That's not what I meant! My heart just about stopped. I said, "I think you should marry me. I think so very strongly."

"And I agree. But what about Mother?"

I said, "What if we took the kneeling part out of the ceremony?"

"Would Father Phillips agree to that? I thought kneeling was very important."

"Father Phillips doesn't want a scene."

"I don't think it's just the kneeling that's getting Mother so upset."

I said, "You're right. It's Christianity. How about if we arrange to see her right afterwards, somewhere else?"

"Would any mother volunteer to miss the wedding of her only child?"

"What if she didn't volunteer?"

"You mean like move to another church and not tell her?"

"Or change the time so we're done before she gets there."

He said, "If this was an *auto-da-fé* we could put a pair of familiars on her. She told me all about this. If she started to misbehave, they would haul her right out."

I burst out laughing. What a hilarious image. The elegant Miriam Beneviste shrieking and thrashing her perfect legs as the thugs dragged her out the doors of the church. I said, "Maybe we could just put her in a straitjacket and a gag and chain her to the pew."

We laughed for a minute. I have been so nervous that my jaw began to ache. I said, "Seriously, what do you think she is going to do?"

"I'm afraid I don't know. This is not the same woman."

"Didn't you talk to her?"

"No. I was too angry."

"You have to."

"I know. I dread it."

"But promise me she won't change your mind about me."

"I promise."

"Promise me you'll be there tomorrow."

"Nothing could stop me. You are my life."

"Kiss me."

He did. He said, "I love you very much."

"Keep thinking that when you talk to your mother."

We kissed again, but my heart was racing, and it didn't feel good. I said, "You will be there?"

He promised again, and I let him go. I walk around and around in my apartment, wondering what Miriam is going to do. Someone help!

204

IF YOU DON'T think I've ever thought much of you, Allison, I hope this proves otherwise. I have breathed an extra half hour just to write these pages for you. Nothing else on this earth could have kept me. They may seem brief and indifferently written, but that's because I cannot close the blistered flesh of my hand.

You must believe that I never objected to you, Allison. It was the Church. Had your union with Solomon been possible without it—which you rejected—I would have been proud to have you in the family. But I could not watch the Church absorb yet one more Beneviste life. You probably think this is mad. Solomon did. But you young people don't understand that we are now floating in a brief calm in a sea of unimaginable violence. It was virtually in my lifetime that we suffered the greatest Inquisition of all. Nobody thought that was possible. Could your goodwill have guaranteed against the next one?

When Solomon came today I intended to convince him of this, right here, in private. I had no intention of causing any more commotion in your lovely church. He insisted on knowing my plans for the day. He was angry. I blessed your wedding just yesterday—did he tell you that?—and he thought I went back on it. That wasn't so. I wanted so hard for you to be happy together that in a weak moment I forgot myself. During the rehearsal I realized I had been wrong, that it could never work out, that the curse of Christ would always hang over us. Solomon slammed his hand on the table and told me that you and he would have the ceremony without me. I was terrified by this rare show of temper, and truly believed that he would leave me behind. I said I would make the wedding impossible if he did not hear me out; if he did, I promised I would not interfere.

What could I say to him that I haven't said many times before? I'm sure you've heard it, our story of drama and horror. Yet today I had to be even more dramatic. I had to finally reach him. Like you, I imagine, I felt time running out.

I brought him down to the basement. He laughed, asking

205

if this was supposed to be his dungeon. It was. I didn't want him laughing. I produced a pair of handcuffs I bought at a novelty store.

He agreed to let me cuff him to a water pipe near the ceiling, provided that I promise to release him in time to dress for the wedding and not to interfere in the service. I had no intention of keeping him away; I wanted to convince him to change his mind. I even put the key to the handcuffs on the floor in front of him so he could see that I fully intended to let him go. I told him that the arguments that he had so blithely rejected would sound different when he was in shackles. He laughed at me again. I said that I had never read of a Beneviste in shackles laughing. We talked again about the church and the history of the family. I suggested that he delay the wedding, since the news of the family past, both ours and yours, has come very rapidly, and he should take time to absorb it. Because this delay might be stressful for him, I offered to take him back into my house. Just until he made his decision, mind you. His answer was: Mama, you're insane.

He didn't use to talk to me this way and I didn't like it. I realized that there was only one thing I could do. I had a skull in my possession, a human skull. When I placed it on the floor in front of Solomon, his mood changed instantly. He wanted to know if it was real, where I got it, who it was, what I was doing. He tried to reach for it, but was held back by his handcuffs. I finally had his attention.

I didn't answer his questions. I let his imagination run. I walked to the garage and waited there a few minutes, as he called after me. Then I returned with the gasoline can that the gardener uses. Now Solomon was straining against his cuffs. I was not sorry to see the cockiness leave him.

I told him that I was surprised he didn't recognize our visitor. He shrieked. Did he know this person? Oh, yes, I told him. Look at the noble shape of the skull, the high brow, the strong jaw. Again he told me I was insane and demanded that I release him. He didn't want any part of this. I told him that's why he was cuffed. He didn't have the gumption to stand here voluntarily. All right, he said, tell me who it is. You can't shock me.

But I could shock him, Allison, and I did. I told him that our visitor was the man who had bought the house for us, so he had every right to return. Solomon stammered. He said, You can't mean Daddy. Why not? I said. He insisted it wasn't so, and I assured him it was (though in fact it was not). He called me a liar. But a minute later he demanded to know whether I'd hidden him away in the attic like some madwoman for twenty-five years. I told him that his father had lain in the ground until just this week. He screamed, Then what is he doing here? I said, He was dug up. I was very calm about it. He cried, You dug Daddy out of his grave? You dug him out of the dirt and took him out of his coffin? You are insane. Let me go! I said I did not dig him up. That wouldn't be right. I had someone else do it for me. There was an olive-skinned laborer happy to take my money. There was hatred in his voice as he told me that I had desecrated the remains of his father, and that his own soul would never know peace again until his father was back in the ground and he had disowned me. I told him that I was glad he felt that way.

Why did I do it? he demanded. I told him that his father had been disinterred because he had judaized. The church would not allow him to escape his accounting simply by dying. Solomon said, Always the church.

I doused the skull with gasoline. Solomon screamed that I was crazy. I struck a match and dropped in on the skull. Flames shot out the eye holes. It was very eerie. Then the skull disappeared into the blaze, only to reappear, dark and ghoulish, from behind the brilliant tongues of fire. Solomon recoiled as far as the handcuffs would allow. He was whimpering, Daddy! Daddy! I said that I had to make him understand what they would do to him, to me, to all of us, if we give them the chance. He had to see how awful it is.

Solomon was tormented by the fire. I decided he had learned his lesson and I could let him go. As I was reaching for the cap to the can, he suddenly kicked at me. The can splattered

207

gasoline all over him, then fell to the floor. I pushed the burning skull away with my foot, but I was not fast enough. The flames raced across the floor. Suddenly my beautiful boy was engulfed in fire.

I leapt on him, trying to extinguish the flames with my hands and my clothing. It didn't work. I had to get him down and roll him. The key to the handcuffs was on the floor. I fell to my knees in the burning gasoline. But I could not find it. I jumped up and tried to wrap myself around him. What else could I do? Calling for help would have taken too long. Water would make the fire worse.

He began to make little gargling noises, so I concentrated on his nose and mouth. The flesh itself was afire, and it stuck to my hands, my son's beautiful skin. He tipped his head up, straining to the full length of his elegant neck. He had a look of horror and fury, just like the Jewish impenitents at the stake. He would not go calmly, like the Christian martyrs.

How long could it have taken? A minute, maybe two. With a final sigh, he sank almost to his knees. Only the cuff was holding him up.

The fire spent itself. I found the key and took my son down and laid him on the floor. He is charred, horrible. I wouldn't know him.

In trying to save him I killed him. I suppose there is some eternal lesson here, but you will have to figure that out. I am not clear-headed now, and don't wish to be.

I don't suppose hearing that I am sorry will mean much to you, Allison. The word "sorry" is so weak. But there is no word for the hideous, wretched revulsion that I feel at myself. Know that I did not mean to take this wonderful man from you, and I would gladly trade places with him. But since I cannot, I will join him. Some day you will come back to life.

Solomon is waiting. I am going to lie down with him and stay beside him forever. Did you know that my Aaron died in my arms? He was in the act of loving me, and collapsed. Maybe I have been wrong to think that my love was any different from the church brand, Allison. In my hands it has been as lethal as it was in the hands of the the Inquisitors. They killed us because they loved us. I killed the only two I ever loved.

The pain is becoming terrific. Before I lose my mobility I am going to leave this journal outside the front door. It is for you. Godspeed. *Adonai Ekhad*.

209

INTERVIEW SHEET

BFI Job Number 62—4013
Fire marshal: M. Hazel

Final remarks: The last entry in the diary of
Miriam Beneviste proves consistent with all
physical evidence and testimony in this
investigation.

For departmental statistical purposes, it is
necessary to determine whether fire was result of
mental pathology.

Interview was held with Dr Elliot, who made
original diagnosis of frontal syndrome as result
of Mrs. Beneviste's head injury. He stated that
he urged Mrs. Beneviste to remain in hospital for
observation, but she insisted on leaving, and he
had no legal right to hold her. He was told that
her skull was now available for his examination,
if that would help him determine her mental state
at time of death. He stated that he might as well
be shown the fragments of a fishbowl and asked
where fish were when it broke.

He was asked whether in his opinion the fire and
deaths were the result of her reaction to the
stresses in her life, or the psychological damage
caused by her injury.

He burst into tears and stated (verbatim), ''I
have no way to answer your question. I am a
doctor, not a minister or a seer. I do not know how

far God's hand reaches to us, or when it does. I
just wish it could reach a little farther a little
more often.''

HELLO DIARY. It's been a whole year. I'm going to air you out a little. I imagine you're stiff and dusty, like me. Look at that—you're ivory colored. I never realized. I figured you for white. I guess I figured everything for white.

Don't think I haven't thought about doing this earlier. I had so much that I wanted to get down in ink. I thought if I could see it on a page maybe it would become more real. But I could never find the words. I kept thinking—Solomon will make sense of all this for me. But he can't. He's dead. He's been dead for a whole year and he's never coming back. I accept it. After a year you can accept things that are completely unacceptable.

I just wish my heart would stop jumping out of my chest every time I see a gray Subaru four-door with aluminum alloy wheels. Doctor Addison says this is natural and it will pass, eventually. Eventually. Is that a nice doctor's way of saying never?

Yesterday I told Doctor Addison that I want to move back to my apartment. He agrees that it's time to return to normal life. (Though I can't even imagine what normal is now.) Mother is going to be furious when I go. She has to remember that she had a life before the fire, and when I leave she can return to it. She doesn't take change well.

You know, Diary, I didn't have to check the date to know it's been a year. Today was the unveiling. Mother and Dad and Jeffrey and I drove up together. It's a really pretty place, landscaped with beautiful flowers and trees, and everything is trim and neat. There is a wonderful view of the river. I would feel very happy for all the people here, if they weren't dead.

Not many living people showed up. It wasn't a surprise, just a disappointment. Solomon's family is tiny, and none of the faithful Episcopalians came, not even the all-forgiving Father Phillips. It was just as well. I put on my sunglasses and held on to Dad's arm and struck an attitude so nobody would come up and talk. I just wasn't in the mood to hear how sorry they were.

A rabbi recited a prayer for the dead in Hebrew. The sounds could have sprung right out of my heart, even though I didn't know the words. Then he said a few things about Solomon and Miriam, how they were good people, hard-working members of the community, and all that. He should have stopped after the prayer. He completely missed the point.

The velvet was pulled from the headstones. I was expecting something that somehow showed what had happened. Instead there were just two slabs of gray marble on the ground, with the names and dates engraved. Everybody started saying how elegant that was, how understated. How wrong.

I wanted to say: People are going see two family stones with the same dates of death and figure it was a car crash or something. And they're going to say—that's a tragedy, but you know, it's the price we pay to be a mobile society. Then they'll walk to the next headstone and see that that family lost a baby who was only six weeks old, and they'll say—what a tragedy, but some babies just don't make it. And Solomon's death will become another garden variety tragedy. But it wasn't. IT WASN'T. I never want people to let themselves off that easily. Solomon died because the world misplaced its heart. That's what they should have engraved on his stone.

All this small talk was infuriating. I was thinking: Somebody say it! It was her fault! She set the fire! Isn't that what you're thinking? You're standing right over their bodies, and what are you saying to each other? My, what a nice day. Good thing we don't have any sons burned to death by their mothers around here. Or mothers who immolated themselves on their sons' bodies. What an unusual color for a geranium.

Maybe I wasn't just thinking it. Because right then Mother said it, so loud that everyone could hear it, even the rabbi. Only she did it with her famous brand of poison. She said, It's disgusting that they put her to rest next to him, after she killed him.

People pretended they didn't hear. Dad said, Good God, hasn't

213

she been punished enough? Mother said, That's not for me to judge. If I was capable of laughter, I would have fallen down from that one.

Every single day for a year I've heard about what the evil Miriam Beneviste did to her son, and to the congregation of the Church of the Ascension. As if that was just as bad! She doesn't even know what really happened. But I do know. I know everything.

Two months ago, when the case was officially over, Detective Chung gave me Miriam's diary. I've read it through every single day. I know Miriam like she lives in my skin. I know Solomon like I gave birth to him. Way better than I did when he was alive. And now, finally, after twenty-nine years, Louise Pennybaker went too far.

I said, Get out. Out of this cemetery.

She thought I was kidding.

I said that it was disgusting that the woman who killed my fiancé could stand over his grave and talk like this.

She said, Kill him? She didn't know what I was talking about. She said I was over-tired. The doctor warned about this. It was time to go home.

I said, It wasn't enough that we were getting married in your church, with your priest, your savior. You had to drain every drop of Jewish blood from him, like he was being sacrificed on some altar. Then you had to go after his mother with your official titles, you licensed body bearer and lay killer. Well, you won, Mother. Why don't you stand right on top of their heathen tombstones. And then get out.

She tried to put a hand to my forehead and I pushed her away hard. I almost knocked her over. That would have been all right with me. I started to scream. Out! All of you, out of this cemetery! The celebration is over. I know people thought I was crazy as a shaved mouse, but I knew what I was doing. Actually, I enjoyed it.

You should have seen them go for their cars. Like the start of the Indy 500. Dad took Mother away. Jeffrey was the only one who came up to me. He said, Don't worry about getting home. I'll swing back for you later.

He knows. I never realized.

So here we are, Diary. Just you and me. Also my wedding veil. Mother stashed it in the attic, but I found it. I knew she wouldn't throw it away. Some day it was going to reappear and wave in my face and remind me about what I mess I made of my life. I'm going to put it on. Easier said than done, Diary, but I succeeded. It's twisted from that fire, and brown. It matches the dirt around your gravestone. Maybe this was the proper color scheme for our wedding. White just wasn't us.

Cold and hard wasn't us either, Solomon. That's how you feel now against my behind. (I've lost a lot of weight. Can you feel the difference?) I wish you could come out and smell the grass and see the view. Even for just a few minutes. Hold my hand. Maybe a kiss.

Doctor Addison would say I shouldn't do this. But he never knew you, Solomon. How could he ever understand how you make me feel. Even now.

Suddenly I feel so tired. I am going to lie down with you, Solomon. Just for a few minutes.

215

I can't believe it. I fell asleep. I could have slept all afternoon if the veil hadn't started blowing into my face.

Miriam is lying next to me, that great shape now just a slab.

Miriam, Miriam, Miriam! We WASPs measure time by the expiration dates on milk cartons. You saw the whole wide long horrible picture. One day I know I will forgive Mother. She is crude and ignorant, but she is basically good. But you? You knew God himself isn't worth my sweet Solomon. And still you took him from me.

My last question is for you, Miriam. Only you can answer. Why don't I hate you? Why was it your diary—not Mother's help or Doctor Addison's advice—that got me through these months? How is it that I love you?

There's a car coming up the drive. It's Jeffrey. He really did come back. I have to finish up now.

Damn. There goes the veil. It's flying toward the river. Well, better that it sinks to the bottom. It was grungy.

I don't think I will come back here. Don't worry, my dark beauties, your tale will be safe in my heart for the rest of my life. But I will never let it consume me.

THE END